Praise for Bruce Gravel's Novels

MW00876443

My Lethal Shadow: *"I thoroughly enjoyed your novella. It was well presented. It kept me completely interested and I was not able to put it down. All the different scenarios and how everything came together at the end. It was great! The thrill of your novella reminds me of some of my favourite writers like Clive Cussler, James Patterson, just to name a few."*
— Marie Poliquin, avid Cussler and Patterson reader

The Hero Stone: *"I stayed up late into the night reading 'The Hero Stone' on my vacation. I was riveted. You got right inside the heads of the three protagonists, including Melanie. The insects and snakes scene was quite compelling!"*
— Colleen Isherwood, Editor, Canadian Lodging News

Inn-Sanity: Diary of an Inn-Keeper Virgin: *"A great read and very interesting. Wow, hard to believe the stories are based on real events!"*
— Kim Litchfield, Corporate Account Manager, WSPS

My
Lethal
Shadow

An action-adventure-romantic-comedy
involving bicycles, a mob daughter, and an assassin

Bruce Gravel

Wigglesworth & Quinn
Peterborough

My Lethal Shadow

Copyright © 2023 by Bruce M. Gravel

For information, contact: bruce@brucegravel.ca.

Published by: Wigglesworth & Quinn, Peterborough, Ontario, Canada
Ordering Information: bruce@brucegravel.ca
Printed in Canada

First Edition: June 2023

Gravel, Bruce M. (Bruce Magnus), 1952 -
    My Lethal Shadow by Bruce Gravel; cover art by Melanie Simpson, Polished Media.

ISBN 9798393982324

   1. Romantic Comedy (English).
   2. Action Adventure (English)

What you can't see...

... can hurt you.

Dedication

To Frances and Scott and Elizabeth
and Isaac,
for their wonderful inspiration, honest feedback,
and constant encouragement.

Books by Bruce Gravel

The "Condiment Series" of short story collections:

Humour on Wry, with Mustard
Humour on Wry, with Mayo
Humour on Wry, with Ketchup
Humour on Wry, with Salsa
Humour on Wry, with Relish
Humour on Wry, with Honey

Novels

Inn-Sanity: Diary of an Innkeeper Virgin
The Hero Stone
My Lethal Shadow

Acknowledgments

The intriguing front cover art was done by **Melanie Simpson** of Polished Media, Toronto, Ontario. Email: melanie@polishedmedia.ca.

Thank you to Frances, Scott and Elizabeth Gravel for their story suggestions.

Special thanks to Frances Gravel, Scott Gravel, and Marie Poliquin for their constructive feedback on the manuscript.

Huge thanks to Frances Gravel for her great job in the formatting and lay-out of the entire book, getting it all print-ready and making it look real pretty.

Many thanks to Scott Gravel for designing the back cover and electronically enabling the printing of the covers.

What a wonderful family affair!

Bruce Gravel
Humourologist turned Rom-Com Writer
April 2023

Where did assassins come from?

"Nothing is true, everything is permitted".

—The Assassin's Creed, from Nietzsche's
Thus Spoke Zarathrusta (1883)

The name "assassin" first came to the West from the Arabic culture.

The founder of the cult of Assassins was a Nizari Ismaili missionary called Hasan-i Sabbah, who infiltrated the castle at Alamut with his followers and bloodlessly ousted the resident king of Daylam in 1090. The Nizari Ismaili were a breakaway group from the Isamaili branch of Shia Islam. The legends of assassins started with this group, which operated in Persia and Syria from the end of the 11th century until the Mongol conquests in the mid-13th century.

The name 'assassin' in English comes from the Latin term assassinus, which is a corruption of the Arabic words hasisi, or hashashin, meaning "hashhish eater". The Nizari Ismailis never used that term for themselves.

Of course, almost every culture had its assassins, some dating back centuries.

The most famous assassin was John Wilkes Booth, who killed President Abraham Lincoln on April 14, 1865, soon after he had won the American Civil War.

Other famous assassins include Lee Harvey Oswald, who killed President John F. Kennedy on November 22, 1963. Nathuram Godse killed Mahatma Gandhi on January 30, 1948. Gavrillo Princip shot Archduke Franz Ferdinand on June 28, 1914, sparking WWI. James Earl Ray assassinated Martin Luther King Jr. on April 4, 1968.

The most feared assassin in history was Julio Santana, a notorious Brazilian hitman considered the deadliest in history for killing 492 people, officially (over 500 unofficially).

"Your identity is like your shadow: not always visible and yet always present.
— Fausto Cercignani

"The brightest flame casts the darkest shadow."
— George RR Martin

"An Assassin, a real Assassin, had to look like one—black clothes, hood, boots, and all. If they could wear any clothes, any disguise, then what could anyone do but spend all day in a small room with a loaded crossbow pointed at the door?"

—**Terry Pratchett,** *Night Watch*

"I NEVER MISS."
—**James Bond,** *The World is Not Enough*

"Do you liken yourself to be an assassin?"
"No," he replied. "I'm just a murderer."

—**'Iceman' Richard Kuklenski,**
the most prolific hitman in Mafia history

"Out, out, brief candle.
Life's but a walking shadow."
—Shakespeare, *Macbeth*

"He that dies
pays all debts."
—Shakespeare, *The Tempest*

Schedule of Events

Chapter One:
The Kidnapping

When I swung aboard my sleek yellow-and-black bicycle that morning, I had no idea my life would soon change forever. It would also be the last time I'd ride that bicycle (which I affectionately called "Bumblebee").

Helmet firmly strapped on, knapsack on my back, and my right pants cuff prudently folded over and held with a velcroed bicycle strap to protect it from the chain, I rode away from my apartment building. I pedaled along a dedicated bicycle lane along the roadside, that passed through pleasant residential neighbourhoods, and which would eventually bring me to downtown Toronto, where I worked. A 45-minute ride, with only a few hills, giving me a nice workout five days a week.

I cycled along at my usual brisk pace, screeching to a stop only when cars shot out from their driveways, their drivers failing to first check for oncoming cyclists. Many of these morons then yelled at me for almost hitting them.

Okay, let's get introductions out of the way: My name is Bernard Keiler. (Don't call me Bernie; I hate that.) I'm 28 years old, currently unattached, living alone in a modest one-bedroom condo apartment. I work at the headquarters of one of Canada's national television networks, as a Senior Technical Director in Master Control. Though my department's name implies something sinister like mind control through the TV airwaves, leading to world domination (which officially only exists in science fiction), my job actually means I ensure the right TV shows get aired at the right time, with—most importantly—the right commercials.

I'm in pretty good shape thanks to riding my bike everywhere (I don't own a car). Still, I always huffed and puffed when going up the steep hill of the aptly-named Hillcrest Street. I crested the hill, anticipating the reward of coasting down the equally-steep other side.

That's when I heard the scream.

Almost halfway down the hill, a black van was parked by the sidewalk. My first thought was that the van inconsiderately squatted across the bicycle lane, which would force me into traffic. Then I looked closer.

On the sidewalk next to the van, in front of an imposing brownstone, two burly men were trying to force a struggling young woman into the open rear double doors of the van. She wore jeans and a blue sweatshirt with a large "U of T" emblazoned across the chest. Her knapsack lay on the sidewalk, but not alone. Two female figures lay sprawled near it, unmoving. Pools of blood were spreading from their bodies onto the concrete.

The woman screamed again. Though she struggled fiercely, the two thugs were inexorably dragging her to the open van doors and the yawning darkness within.

Jumbled thoughts coursed through my brain. *Am I the only one seeing this?* Apparently so. *Do I stop and call 911?* The kidnappers would be long gone before the police could arrive. *Do I try and follow the van, hopefully noting its licence plate number?* The van's speed would soon outdistance even my best pedaling efforts and I knew from watching countless TV shows, that it would soon be ditched for another vehicle, making the licence number useless.

So what was I to do? I had to do something. The young woman was almost inside the van.

I suddenly realized that I was rocketing down the hill. While I had been focused on the drama in front of me, gravity was doing what gravity did best.

Anyone who knows me would tell you that I'm not a brave man. I'm certainly not an aggressive man. So thoughts of single-handedly effecting a rescue were not in my mind at the moment.

Instead, my brain screamed: *Brake! Brake! Brake! You're gonna hit them, you idiot!*

I was now almost at the van, traveling very fast, the wind and the whirring of my wheels a crescendo in my ears. I was heading right for the two kidnappers and their prey. Targeting the woman in the middle, in fact.

That's when the trio noticed me.

Three sets of mouths opened in horror. Three sets of arms came up, crossing over in front of their faces (the criminals had released their grips on their captive at the sight of my imminent crash into them). Four sets of screams sounded (I was the fourth).

At the last second, I swerved from the woman and aimed at the thug on the right. I plowed into him at full speed, my beautiful $3,000 bicycle mashing into his body and the van door behind.

I later found out that the university student excelled in track & field. She used her quick reflexes and powerful leg muscles to launch herself backwards into the very place she had been fighting to stay out of: the van. This saved her from my onslaught. It also cleared the airspace.

I don't know how I did it, but as I crashed into the kidnapper, I somehow flung myself off my bike, pinwheeling with arms and legs akimbo into the thug on the left.

The force of my impact knocked the man away from the left rear door and into the roadway. Where he was promptly hit by a speeding Mercedes.

Meanwhile, I heroically smashed my head into the van's bumper. Everything went black.

When I came to, I was lying on a Gurney with flashing lights all around. A paramedic was fussing with my head, which hurt like hell.

I heard sobbing and turned my head, annoying the paramedic trying to treat me. It was the woman, sitting on the rear ledge of the ambulance with a blanket around her shoulders. She was crying into her hands.

A person came into my view and introduced herself as Detective Kate Millard. She wanted to question me about my involvement.

Detective Millard already had my name and address from my wallet, which someone had taken from my pocket while I lay unconscious. In a weak, quavering voice that I did not recognize, I told her what happened. She took notes.

"So you single-handedly incapacitated both of the lady's kidnappers, Mr. Keiler," she said when I had finished. "Quite the Good Samaritan."

I grinned; it hurt. "I really didn't know what I was doing. It all happened so fast," I said.

"Well, that young woman is safe, thanks to you," she said. "One of the kidnappers is dead —the one you knocked into the Mercedes. The other man, the one you ran your bike into, is in a coma with severe internal injuries from where your handlebars rammed his stomach. Your front tire crunching into his privates didn't do him any favours either. We plan to question him when he awakens."

"Ah, and my bike? It's quite expensive, you know. It's my one luxury."

"It's now an expensive tangle of scrap metal, is what it is," she replied, then added a somewhat-sympathetic afterthought. "Sorry."

I craned my head and saw the twisted mess of yellow and black metal. *Bumblebee!* I felt like crying.

Then I wondered if an art gallery would buy it, as a

modern sculpture. *Hazardous Commuting*, by Someone Famous. It would help pay for a new bike.

I looked past the bike and saw two black body bags on the sidewalk.

"The two women I saw lying on the sidewalk?" I asked. She nodded.

"They're both dead?" I asked. She nodded.

"They were the student's bodyguards," Millard said. "The kidnappers shot them, then grabbed her. You know what happened next. She's crying because she's very attached to them; both women had been guarding her since she was a little girl."

"Wait, what? Bodyguards?" I said. "What kind of university student needs bodyguards?"

"So you have no idea who you just saved?" she asked.

I shook my head, then moaned as pain shot through it. It felt like somebody was hitting an anvil inside there.

"Okay, enough questions for now," the paramedic said sternly. "He's going to the hospital for a complete check-up, including an MRI. He likely has a concussion."

The paramedic looked at me. "If you hadn't been wearing a helmet, my friend, it would have been much worse."

I looked down at my helmet, lying on the street where

the paramedic had dropped it after cutting it off. A deep crack disfigured the top.

"Okay, we'll talk more another time," Detective Kate said, waving me off.

It was only the next day that I learned whose daughter that woman was.

Chapter Two:
The Summons

I was in hospital for three days, enduring innumerable tests and the hospital food. My first day, one hour after being deposited in a semi-private room, I was abruptly moved into a private room.

"But the medical plan I have with my employer only covers semi-private," I protested. "I can't afford private."

"It's all been taken care of," said the nurse. "In fact, anything you want—anything at all unless it conflicts with doctor's orders—is covered. All you have to do is ask. For starters, you have full access to all TV channels and high speed Internet."

After she left, I concluded they had me mixed up with somebody else. I hurt too much to complain.

That evening, I watched the news on my network's station, while trying to decide what was worst: starving or eating what was supposed to be my dinner. That morning's attempted kidnapping was the lead story, adhering to the old media adage: "If it bleeds, it leads". The ever-perky Brittany, our evening news desk personality, informed viewers that the young lady I had saved was Dominique Vargas, 23-year-old daughter and only child of the alleged crime czar of eastern Canada. In deference to our network's lawyers, Brittany hastily added that any such allegation was unproven, and smiled her million-dollar artificially-whitened smile.

I choked and almost spewed out the alien porridge-like substance I had finally decided to eat.

Holy crap! She's Vargas' daughter! Well, that explained the bodyguards.

After dwelling on the dead people, and possible motives for the kidnapping, the newscast finally did a small piece on the so-called hero rescuer. There was my photo from work and a heartbreaking shot of my mangled *Bumblebee*. The wreckage got more air time than my face. Brittany got my name and job title correct, which amazed me, as I believed no one in the other network departments knew of, or cared about, us drones in Master Control.

I was a little miffed that no video journalist had come to interview me. *I'm a hero, dammit! Said so on the news.*

At 9:00 next morning, a gigantic bouquet of flowers arrived. The attached note card stated: "Thank you so much for saving me." It was signed "Dominique". She had underlined the word "so". She had nice cursive handwriting —rare among students these days.

Around 10:30 a.m., I was surprised when two reporters showed up. One was from a daily Toronto newspaper, the other from my network. This latter was an intern fresh out of college, eager to please, but woefully green. I was miffed again, this time because I had not been deemed worthy of an experienced reporter.

After the video journalist had set up his camera and

invasively attached an almost-hidden mike to my hospital gown, both reporters asked me a barrage of questions. I kept my answers short; being in the business, I knew reporters only wanted five-to-ten second sound bites to edit into their story.

"So you had no idea who you were saving?" one asked.

"None whatsoever," I replied. "She was just someone in trouble."

"Who was trying to kidnap her?"

"No idea. The police are still working on that."

"How do you feel about saving the daughter of a notorious organized crime baron?"

"I saved a human being, a terrified young woman. Anyone would have done the same."

"What kind of specialized combat training do you have, to do what you did?"

"I play a lot of *Fortnite* and *Call of Duty* video games."

"Is our city safe? Must people worry about gang warfare?"

"I don't think our city is any more dangerous than other cities. Crime can happen anywhere."

"What happens for you now?"

"I get better, then I must look for a new bike. It's how I get around, including commuting to work. My former ride is scrap metal."

"So you're an environmentalist? You believe in climate change, global warming? Do you support the Green Party?"

"I'm just a guy who enjoys riding his bike everywhere."

The evening news carried my interview, which was mostly accurate, though the news writers had slanted it into a condemnation of the increased violence in our city, which Brittany faithfully read to the cameras.

Next day, the paper carried much the same story. These days, with two or three mega-corporations owning multiple news outlets, as soon as one story was written, everyone else simply repeated it.

The following day, I was discharged with a vial of painkillers for my still-throbbing head, and a prescription for more when the vial ran out. Except for a mild concussion, scratches, and some spectacular bruises, I was otherwise healthy. Still, the doctor advised me to take it easy for the next few days.

I was wearing the same clothes I'd worn the morning of the crash, now torn, wrinkled and stained. I looked like a street person (with apologies to street persons). I didn't have anyone to bring me fresh clothes from my apartment.

I donated my huge floral display to the nurses' station, and asked if they could please call a cab to take me home.

I was told transportation had already been arranged, and was waiting for me at the front doors.

"Oh? By who?" I asked. They didn't know.

I stopped by the billing office on my way out, to confirm I didn't owe them anything. While our provincial health plan paid for most medical care, it didn't cover any extras like private or semi-private rooms, TV, etc. I was assured my bill had been paid in full.

"Oh? By who?" I asked. They didn't know.

A highly-polished burgundy Lincoln Town Car awaited me outside the front doors, parked in a No Stopping zone. A smiling uniformed chauffeur stood next to the car. If he disapproved of how I looked, he didn't show it. He opened the rear door as I approached.

"My name is Thomas and I'll be your driver," he said. "Please get in."

"Um, I'm Bernard Keiler. Is this ride really for me?"

"Indeed it is, Sir," the chauffeur beamed.

I slid onto the soft leather seat. The door clicked shut. Walking around the car and slipping behind the wheel, Thomas eased us into city traffic.

"Wow, this car rides so smooth," I said. "And it's so quiet inside here."

"Would you care for some music?" Thomas asked. "I can

play any type you want; this car has Sirius."

"Of course it does. Um, your choice." Light jazz came over the perfectly-modulated speakers. That was good; with my head, I couldn't handle rock.

We pulled in front of a high-end men's clothing store. The only thing in that store that fit my budget was the right to stand outside and drool at their window display.

"Why are we stopping here?" I asked.

"To get you more presentable clothing. You look like a street person—with apologies to street persons," said Thomas.

"Just drive me home. I've lots of fresh clothes there."

"Not an option, Sir."

Ignoring my protests, he courteously, but firmly, ushered me into the store. The owner himself, and two assistants, served us. In a surprisingly short time, I was dressed in a complete new outfit: slacks, belt, fitted silk shirt, jacket, socks, and handmade Italian leather shoes. All of which fit me perfectly. When I complained that I couldn't afford these clothes—the shoes alone cost what I made in a month—I was assured it would all be taken care of.

The owner gave me a paper bag containing my old clothes and shoes, after first asking if he should simply incinerate them.

"No. The tears can be stitched and the stains can be washed. They're good clothes. I bought 'em at Walmart."

The haberdasher did not sniff in distaste, but I could tell he wanted to.

Back in the car, we drove up the entrance ramp to the elevated expressway that straddled the city.

"Who hired you to drive me?" I said.

"No one," Thomas chuckled. "This is one of my employer's cars."

I was about to ask who his employer was, when I noticed something.

"Hey, um, you just passed the exit for my street," I said. "You'll have to take the next exit and double back."

"Oh, we're not going to your apartment," he said, glancing at me in his rear view mirror. "We're going for a drive in the country."

"I don't want a drive in the country!" I protested. "I just wanna go home."

"My employer wishes to see you," he said, with the finality of a judge handing down a sentence.

I should have realized it before now, but in my own defense, I had been dealing with painful head trauma:

I had an awful feeling I knew who his employer was.

Chapter Three:
The Debt

We drove for about 40 minutes, taking us out of Toronto and its suburbs, and into rolling farmland and woodlands.

We stopped in front of a massive wrought iron gate. Thomas removed his cap and sunglasses and stared at a small screen mounted to a pole by the gate. I read the word "confirmed" on the screen, then the tall gates ponderously swung open.

"Facial recognition?" I said.

"Yes," he replied. "Your picture was taken too, by a camera on the opposite side of the car." I noticed he had lowered the heavily-tinted rear passenger window.

We drove up a long, winding driveway, bordered by manicured shrubs, trees, and flower beds. We pulled up in front of a sprawling mansion that put movie stars' mansions to shame, and stopped.

"Wow," I breathed.

"Indeed. And wait'll you see inside," said Thomas.

He came around the car and opened my door.

"Come in," he said, waving his arm at the mansion.

"Do I have a choice?" I said.

"Not at all, Sir."

An imposing oak door silently opened as we approached the entrance. The wood was carved into a beautiful underwater seascape.

Entering, I found myself in a cavernous foyer, with a soaring ceiling, marble floor, and a wide marble staircase curving gracefully—like a swan's neck—to a second floor. A substantial colourful Chihuly glass sculpture hung from the ceiling.

"Wow," I said.

"Indeed," Thomas said.

"I see why you wanted me to change clothes."

"Indeed."

He led me down a long wide corridor to another big oak door at the end. This one was carved with horses running wild, manes and tails streaming behind.

I was ushered into a gigantic office. Floor to ceiling glass windows made up one entire wall, overlooking a professionally-landscaped backyard sloping gently to a sparkling river. The other walls were occupied with a mix of bookcases, and paintings that looked to be all originals. The furniture was all carved wood. The carpeting was lush.

I thought my entire apartment could fit in there.

A large carved teak desk was in the precise centre of the wall of windows. A high-back leather chair was behind the desk, but facing the windows. I could tell the chair was occupied, as it moved slightly.

I gulped. *Omigod! That's him! The crime czar of half of Canada! Vargas! The Godfather!* I broke out in a cold sweat, stifling a whimper. I wondered how far I'd get if I turned and ran away.

"Mister Bernard Keiler, ma'am," said the chauffeur.

Ma'am?

"Thank you, Thomas," replied a definitely-not-male voice.

The chair swung around and I was staring at a woman. Jet black hair, cut short in an aggressive style. Long, perfectly-made-up face with high cheekbones. She looked to be in her early fifties. She rose and came around the desk. She wore a beautifully-tailored light grey business suit and a white blouse. She stretched out her hand. Numbly, I shook it.

"A pleasure to meet you, Mr. Keiler," she said. "The man who saved my daughter."

"Ah, thanks," I managed. "P-please call me Bernard. I-I was expecting—"

"A man?"

She smiled a thin-lipped smile and returned to her

chair. She had a lean figure and walked with a lithe grace that reminded me of panthers I'd seen in nature documentaries.

"Please take a seat," she said.

Nervous, I perched on the edge of one of the two ornate chairs in front of her desk.

"Relax," she said.

I moved an inch deeper into the chair.

She smiled again. "My name is Angelica Vargas. Only a select few may call me by my first name. You are now one of them."

"Uh, th-thanks, um, Angelica. Sorry about assuming you'd be male. I assumed I would be meeting Mr. Vargas."

"Mr. Vargas was my father. I raised Dominique as a single mother."

I nodded. She waited for me to say something. When I did not, she continued:

"I trust the drive out here was pleasant? And your hospital stay and new clothes are satisfactory?"

"Y-yes," I stammered. "So it was you who paid for all that stuff?"

"It was. A trifle, considering what you did for my family."

"Th-thank you for your generosity, but there—there was no need."

"There was. You have rendered me a great favour by stopping the kidnapping of my only child. I am in your debt. And I always pay my debts."

"You—you already paid for these clothes and my hospital bill," I said.

"As I said, a trifle. Bernard, you deserve a substantial reward for your heroic actions. Dominique means more to me than anything I possess."

"I'm just glad she's okay. Do you have any idea who was behind the kidnapping? The cops are still figuring that out."

"I have resources unavailable to the police," she said. "I know exactly who was behind the attempted kidnapping."

I looked at her expectantly. She continued: "Very well, you deserve to know. The kidnappers work for a foreign enterprise that is trying to supplant my business interests. Unlike us, they have no honour, no code of ethics. They involve innocents, like my daughter, to get what they want.

"They surprised her and her bodyguards outside my city townhouse, where Dominique stays to attend university. If they had succeeded in taking her, their demands for her safe return would have crippled my businesses. And after they received what they wanted from me, they would have killed Dominique anyway, after she first suffered through unimaginable tortures. These people are animals.

"So I trust you now understand the magnitude of what you did, saving her—saving us. Now I must repay you for your heroism, your service to me."

She named a figure that left me speechless. "Simply provide me with your bank account number, and it will be deposited first thing tomorrow."

"What? No—no, I couldn't, I shouldn't."

"Well then, if not money, how about an exotic car? Maserati, Ferrari, or even a McLaren? There's a new model McLaren out."

"No—no, I—"

"How about a detached house in one of Toronto's best neighbourhoods? Or a villa on the French Riviera, or on St. Barts in the Caribbean?"

I gawped at her, speechless.

"Do close your mouth, Bernard. You resemble a codfish."

I finally found my voice. "With all due respect, ma'am— ah, Angelica—I don't want anything. I'm happy I managed to save your daughter, and I'm happy she's unharmed. That's good enough for me."

Angelica leaned forward, placing her hands on her desk. "It is not good enough for me. I owe you a great debt, which must be repaid. It is a matter of honour."

She gave me an unblinking stare. "It is because of who I

am, is it not? That is why you will not accept anything from me."

"Well, please forgive me, but you do have a fearsome reputation."

"It is all vicious rumours," she said, an icy edge to her voice. "I run many highly-profitable legitimate businesses. But because I am a woman operating in a man's world, they label me with nasty titles. Completely disrespectful. Very hurtful.

"After my father died, 12 years ago, I have run the family businesses even better than he did, growing them and generating far more profit than he ever did. But because I am a woman, I have had to work twice as hard, to achieve that success."

"I—I didn't mean to imply —"

"Yes you did. Typical male. I am merely a very successful businesswoman, no matter what you hear."

She leaned back into her chair. "And I owe you a debt that must be paid."

Inspiration struck me. "Okay, then give me five dollars and we'll call it paid."

Angelica went very still. "You think my Dominique's life is only worth five dollars? How *dare* you! That is an insult!"

Two large, burly men entered the room through a silent sliding door between two bookcases, and came towards me.

"No, that's not what I meant at all!" I squeaked. "I was just trying to reach an agreement with you! I meant no disrespect!"

She raised a hand. The two men stopped.

"You are fortunate I am so very grateful for what you did," she said, the anger slowly leaving her voice. "People who insult me never do so again. So, back to our business: what can I give you, to repay my debt to you?"

"Just —just have your driver take me home. Please. That is what I want. Just to go home. My head really hurts."

She regarded me for long seconds. "All right. If that is what you want, Bernard. Again, please accept my thanks for what you did."

She waved a dismissive hand. Wordless, the two goons led me back to the front door, one in front of me and one behind. When I exited the mansion, Thomas and his gleaming Lincoln were waiting in the circular drive.

"I really hope you're going to take me home this time," I said.

"Absolutely, Sir."

We drove back into the city and to my apartment, with soft jazz the only sound. My breathing only returned to normal halfway there, when I became convinced Thomas wasn't taking me to a remote forest, where my grave would never be found.

Now I knew how the mouse felt in that fable about the mouse and the lion. Angelica radiated power; elegant cold power.

I barely registered getting changed and crawling into bed. I was asleep before my head hit the pillow.

I woke up late and took a long, hot shower. Emerging from the bathroom in a cloud of steam, I padded to the livingroom, holding a towel around my hips. I stopped abruptly.

A man dressed in black was sitting on my couch. There was a black handgun on my coffee table in front of him, with silencer attached.

"Who —who the hell are you?" I demanded.

"I'm the greatest assassin you've never heard of," he replied. His voice dripped oil. "Ms. Vargas sent me to you, to settle a debt."

My towel dropped to the floor.

Chapter Four:
The Gift

I pride myself at keeping my head in stressful situations. It's one reason why I excel at my job at Master Control at the TV network. When everyone else is wailing, swearing, and losing their minds over a programming or technical glitch, steady ol' Bernard can be counted on to solve the problem.

So you can imagine how I handled finding a black-clad assassin in my livingroom.

"AAAAH!" I screamed. "Don't shoot me! PleaseGodpleasedon'tkillme!"

The man in black looked me up and down.

"Well, my pistol is bigger than yours," he said. "Now just calm down, Bernie. Pick up your towel and sit yourself down. We gotta talk."

Realizing I was stark naked, I hastily did as he asked. Heart pounding, I looked at him. A lean man, with a long face of thin lips, hawk nose, and piercing blue eyes. His black hair was up swept into a forward-leaning point. His clothes—jacket, shirt, pants, shoes—were as black as his hair. If the Grim Reaper wore a human body, it would look like him.

"Y-you're here to—to kill me, right?" I quavered.

"Wrong. I'm not here to kill you. I'm here to kill *for* you."

"Wh-what?"

"Yup, this is your lucky day, Bernie boy. Ms. Vargas is in your debt big time, an' apparently what she offered you yesterday didn't float your boat. An' may I say, you were batshit crazy to refuse the rewards she dangled in front of you. Anyway, so here we are: I'm your gift, from her to you."

"Wh-what?"

"Bit slow on the uptake, Bernie? Oh, right, I remember the briefing: you got whacked on the head something fierce. Lemme try and make it clear:

"I'm an assassin, okay? One of the best. To pay her debt to you, Ms. Vargas hired me to kill whomever you want, no questions asked. I can do it quick an' clean, or slow an' messy. Making it look like an accident is my specialty.

"Anyone you want. A boss that's pissing you off, an asshole neighbour, an ex-wife or girlfriend, a family member busting your chops. Just name him or her, an' leave the rest to me. Nothing will ever be traced back to you. Guaranteed."

I stared at him, speechless.

"Hello? Anyone home? Okay, I suspect suddenly seeing me here might have flustered you a bit. Let's start again:

"Hi, you can call me Oliver. You're Bernie Keiler. Tell me who you want dead. Um, please."

"First off, it's Bernard. I hate being called Bernie," I finally said.

"No problem, Bernie."

"Second, there's no way I'm pointing you at anyone, to kill them. That's awful, inhuman! It would also make me an accessory to murder!"

"Like I said, it'll never be traced back to you, 'specially if I make it look like an accident. See, Bernie, it's real important to Ms. Vargas that she settle this debt she owes you. She's not someone you wanna trifle with. Trust me on that. I've been hired quite a few times to resolve a situation for her. Though I will admit, never like this, giving someone *carte blanche* to use me to kill whomever they want. So don't piss around. Give me a name, I get it done, an' Ms. Vargas will be happy. You don't want her angry at you."

Remembering our encounter in her office yesterday, when she was quick to take offense at my five dollar suggestion, I nodded.

"So c'mon, there must be somebody you want dead, somebody who's really pissed you off, or threatens your life, or whatever," Oliver said. "Like, how about your boss? Everybody hates their boss."

"Yeah, I do hate him. Sanctimonious bastard. Knows half of what I do, but lords it over me as if I was a green intern. He's blocked my promotion at least twice."

"Perfect." Oliver pulled out a small black notebook and a black pen from one of his black pockets. "Give me his name."

"I don't hate him enough to kill him!" I exclaimed. *At least not yet.*

"Sounds to me like you have plenty of reasons to want him iced."

"Yes—but no."

"Okay, how about a co-worker? Someone who got that promotion you were counting on, someone who's always sucking up to the boss."

"Yeah, there's two of those among my colleagues."

Oliver flipped open his notebook. "Name of the worst one? Unless you want to pay me to do the second one too? I'd give you a special price."

"No! I detest them, but I don't want to sentence them to death!"

"Well, how about the guy who stole your wife, or girlfriend? I know you're currently unattached, but you must have had a significant other. Give me the name of the bastard who stole her away."

"Um, it wasn't like that. We broke up by mutual agreement seven months ago. She's seeing someone else now, but that relationship started after we broke up."

"You sure?"

"Yeah."

"Damn. Say, on a related topic, you had a date since your break-up?"

"Um, no. But I've been trying!"

He whistled. "No date in seven months! Look, Bernie, I'll do you a favour. Lemme give you a few dating tips. I've dated plenty of women—they're attracted to me. Many women like a scoundrel."

"Right. I'm so desperate that I'm now getting dating tips from a cold-blooded killer? No thanks! And no offense."

"None taken—lucky for you. Just tryin' to help. Okay, back to business. What about a neighbour? Lots of people can't stand their neighbours."

He must have seen something in my face. He said triumphantly: "Ah ha! I just hit paydirt!"

"Yeah, the guy living above me always plays his music way too loud, late at night. Lots of thumping on his floor—my ceiling—sometimes so hard it rattles my ceiling lights."

"Perfect. Name, please."

"While it's true I can't stand him, I can't have him murdered over some noise!"

"Why not?" Oliver purred in a low voice. "It's chronic noise, disturbing your peaceful enjoyment of your home, your sanctum. Lots of people are killed for less. Just gimme his name, an' you'll enjoy peace again."

"No!"

Oliver made an exasperated sound, flipping his notebook shut. "You're stubborn as hell."

"Not the first time I've heard that."

I looked at his gun lying on my coffee table. Cold black deadly metal. "Why's your gun there?"

"It's one of the tools of my trade. I put it there to convince you I'm who I say I am. I wanted you to take me seriously."

I had never seen a handgun up close. I swallowed and said: "Well, if you really must kill something, there's a psychotic dog across from my balcony that barks all day and most of the night. Drives me crazy."

"No can do, Bernie. I don't kill dogs," he said. "Or old ladies. Professional ethics."

"A hitman with ethics," I said.

"Everyone has a line they will not cross, Bernie. I loved my dog growing up. An' my Ma is an old lady. Taught me the family business."

"Your—your mother is an assassin?" I asked.

"Was. She's retired now. In her day, she was one of the best. So sweet and kind. No one ever suspected her. She could kill you in a hundred different ways, with a smile on her face.

"My dad was her first victim. He abused her terribly, but when he started on me when I was eight, she had enough. She arranged a lethal accident, that fooled the cops. Work of art, it was." Oliver sighed.

"I wondered how one learned to be an assassin," I said. "I wondered if there was a school somewhere."

"Actually, there is. Some countries have one. They're run by their governments, and the graduates must then work for those governments. Killing whomever they're told to kill, even whole families, no questions asked. That's certainly not for me. I enjoy being freelance."

"By the way, how did you even get into my apartment?" I demanded.

"Picking locks is another skill," he replied. "Thanks again to dear ol' Mum. You really should invest in a dead bolt, or at least a security chain."

"Listen—Oliver—I didn't want any of the rewards Angelica offered me yesterday, and there's no way I want your services either. I want no part of somebody's murder! Besides being morally and legally wrong, it's paid by dirty money—mob money! I want no part of it!"

Oliver regarded me, his stare unblinking. Then he leaned forward and said in a grave-cold voice:

"Look, Bernie, you fail to understand something about

all this. It's all about honour. Ms. Vargas is honour-bound to repay you for the debt you've placed upon her. I am honour-bound to fulfill my contract with her. Once I take a contract, I always complete it. Always. It's one of the things I'm known for. Professional ethics.

"So the ball is in your court, buddy. You must give me a name and I must terminate that person. Only then will my contract be satisfied. Only then will Ms. Vargas' debt with you be settled. Do you understand, Bernie?"

"Don't. Call. Me. Bernie," I said. "My name is Bernard."

I stood up. "I've had quite enough of you. Get the hell out of my home!"

Oliver unfolded his lanky frame from the couch. He towered over me, being over six feet. He picked up his gun. I gulped.

He unscrewed the silencer, placing it in a jacket pocket. Then he placed his gun in a shoulder holster, hidden by his jacket.

He smiled at me. There was no humour in that smile. "Okay, I'll go. But you have not seen the last of me. Bernie."

Chapter Five:
The Delivery

The next day, I went to a hardware store and bought a dead bolt lock for my apartment door, plus a security chain for good measure. The dead bolt lock instructions promised, in both official languages, that it would only take 20 minutes to install.

It took me two hours.

Afterwards, I phoned my TV network's Human Resources department to discuss my return to work.

"So I'm talking to a real live action hero," said Armintha, the HR supervisor. "Why are you anxious to return to work?"

"Because staying home is driving me crazy," I replied.

"Why? Isn't it relaxing?" she asked.

Finding a contract killer sitting on your livingroom couch isn't my definition of relaxing. I said: "Not as much as you'd think."

"Well, you hardly ever take any sick days, Bernard. So why not stay home another week and enjoy the break?

"No thanks. I want to get back to my normal life."

"Suit yourself."

She scheduled me to return to work in two days. Being bereft of *Bumblebee*, I started researching public transportation to get me into work.

I also called my insurance agent, to see if I could claim my smashed $3,000 bike on my policy. Since I had deliberately caused the crash, regardless of my Good Samaritan motives, she told me my claim would be denied. She encouraged me to have a nice day, then the line went dead.

I resolved to do two things: 1.) Visit my bike shop tomorrow to see if they had a payment plan for a replacement cycle. 2.) Shop for a new insurance provider when my current policy came due.

The next day, as I was cleaning up the detritus of a late breakfast, my door buzzer buzzed. This was an intercom connecting the front foyer with individual apartments. If the callee approved of the caller, then they could buzz them into the building through the foyer's locked inner door.

So Oliver the assassin got through that door too, I realized.

I pressed the intercom button. "Yes?"

A gruff male voice informed me I had a delivery.

"I'm not expecting a delivery," I said.

"Well, ya got one anyway, bud. Can I bring it up?"

My inner voice cautioned: *Careful! He could have a thermonuclear suitcase bomb, or a crank delivery of fifteen pizzas.* Ignoring the voice, which always sounded like my late mother, I buzzed him in.

Minutes later, there was a knock on my door. Releasing my new locks, I opened the door and gasped.

A gorgeous young woman stood there with a shiny new yellow-and-black bicycle!

"Hi Bernard," she said, a little shyly. "We've met—sorta. I'm Dominique Vargas."

I stared at her. She was dressed in black yoga pants and a tight green t-shirt with "There is no Planet B" stenciled across the front. Her reddish-brown hair was tied in a ponytail. She wore no make-up.

"Well, um, this is for you. My thank-you for saving me," she said. "You need a new bike."

Dumbstruck, I took hold of the bike. She followed me as I wheeled it into my livingroom.

"I left my new bodyguards in the lobby," she said. "Um, how are you feeling? I know you got pretty banged up saving me. You doing okay?"

"Yeah, getting better."

I realized with shock that I was wearing my ratty old PJs and my equally-ratty old dressing gown. My uncombed hair looked like a bird's nest. *Gah! That's twice she's seen me at my worst!*

I propped the bike against the wall. It was a higher-end high-performance bicycle than *Bumblebee* had been: a Cervelo R5. It had an ultra-lightweight carbon fibre frame that was aerodynamically superb. The machine screamed SPEED. This bike was easily worth $6,500, more than twice what *Bumblebee* had cost.

"Wow," I breathed.

"So you like it?" Dominique asked.

"Oh yes. But I can't accept this."

"I know you turned down my mother's offers, but this is not from her," she said sharply. "It's from me. I paid for it, with my money. It's the least I can do for what you did."

"The ... the least?" I stammered.

She chuckled. "No, not the least. Bernard, I want to take you to dinner sometime. I want to get to know the man who saved my life."

She suddenly smiled, a glorious breathtaking smile.

"And I don't take no for an answer. I'm like my mother that way."

Then she turned and swept out my open door into the hall. I stepped out and watched her walk down the hallway to the elevator. She had a very nice figure. She turned and waved before stepping into the elevator.

There was a soft click behind me. I whirled, staring. My door had closed and latched shut.

I didn't have my key with me.

Eventually, I regained access to my apartment. (Dressed as I was, I'd had to clump down to the building manager's office in the basement, to have her let me in using the duplicate key I'd given her yesterday. Most embarrassing.)

I changed into my riding gear, made some adjustments on the bike to suit my height and leg length, then headed out to give it a practice spin. I rode slowly through my neighbourhood, and the next two neighbourhoods, favoring my injuries. The Cervelo handled like a dream. *Bumblebee* had been a Cadillac. The new bike was a Rolls Royce, but with the performance of a Ferrari at Le Mans. I couldn't wait to go fast on it. *(Do I name this one* Bumblebee II*?)*

Heading back home, I stopped at a red light. Several young men were hanging out on the street corner. They quickly noticed my distinctive bike. Appreciative comments came my way.

"Ya better keep a close eye on that beauty, my man," said one guy, grinning. "It's one sweet ride."

I smiled back, the light changed, and I took off again.

Reaching home, I brought the bike into the basement to the bike storage area provided for the condo owners. The storage area, with floor-to-ceiling chain-link fencing, had a common lock on the door, to which us cyclists had the combination. Prudently, I also locked my bike to an interior stand that was bolted to the floor. Ironically, it was the same spot where *Bumblebee* had been locked.

Back upstairs in my apartment, I was reading through the bike's detailed owner's manual, when an uneasy feeling swept over me. I fired up my laptop and researched the Cervelo high-performance bicycle manufacturing company. It took me almost an hour to dig through all the layers.

Though a Canadian company, Cervelo was actually part of a consortium of companies owned by an offshore holding company, registered in the Bahamas. It was a privately-held company that did not disclose its officers or its financial reports. It, in turn, was owned by a larger privately-held holding company, registered in Switzerland.

After piercing layers of lawyers, accountants, managing directors, and public relations personnel, I discovered the Swiss holding company was solely owned by a Ms. A. Vargas, a Canadian.

Her again!

I was in a quandary: Do I refuse the bike, knowing it came from one of her businesses? Or do I keep it, since her daughter had bought it and the bike company was a legitimate Canadian business, with no hint of mob involvement?

I stared at the owner's manual. *What should I do?*

My mother's voice in my head said: *Refuse it.*

My heart said: *Keep it.*

Sighing, I went with my heart. *Suck it up, Mom.*

The next morning would render my mental debate irrelevant.

Chapter Six:
The Theft

I passed a restless night. Tossing, turning, staring at the ceiling. *Should I keep that bike? It's a gift from her daughter, but isn't it ultimately from her mother? It comes from dirty money. Mob money.*

But if I refuse it, I have no bike. I wrecked Bumblebee *saving Dominique. Isn't it fair that she replaces the bike I lost?*

I finally fell into a fitful sleep. My last thought: *Am I a hypocrite?*

Next morning, I woke earlier than usual. I showered and dressed in the snazzy outfit Angelica had bought me. It was my first day back at work, and I wanted to impress my fellow minions. Hey, I'm only human.

As I looked myself over in the mirror, I wondered if wearing her clothes was also hypocritical.

Yes, said my motherly conscience.

Oh, shut up, stupidhead, said my brain.

After drinking a breakfast smoothie, I took the elevator to the basement and walked to the bicycle storage area. At this early hour, there was no one around. I wanted to leave early, because I would pedal to work slower than usual. I didn't know how my body would handle the 45 minute ride; I was still sore in many places.

I came around a corner and saw the bike area. I stopped, mouth agape. The usually-locked chain-link door was open, hanging drunkenly on its one remaining twisted hinge. The other hinge was broken. The door lock was shattered.

I ran inside. My brand-new $6,500 cycle was gone. It's lock, supposedly unbreakable, that had bound it to the bike rack, lay on the floor, cut off.

There were some other empty bike racks, which should have been occupied at this hour, with their locks also lying cut on the cement floor.

I don't believe this! What had I done to deserve such bad luck?

"AUGH!" I screamed. "Goddammit! I didn't even have that bike for 24 hours! I'll kill the asshole who stole it!"

A low voice spoke from the shadows: "I'll take care of him for you."

"WAAA!" I yelled and whirled around. Oliver sauntered into the light. He was still dressed completely in black.

"You scared the living crap outta me!" I shouted.

"You scare easily," said the man in black. "Thanks for finally giving me a target. I know the local gang who did this. So do you; you talked with them yesterday during your little bike ride."

"Wha-?"

"Yup. I been keeping an eye on you. Their leader—the guy who talked to you—took your bike, while his boys snagged the others. A bike that expensive, you really shoulda kept it inside your apartment."

"How ... how the hell did you get in here?" I demanded.

"Same way the gang did: wait until someone goes out and grab the door before it closes. Easy. It's how I got into your building's lobby the day we met."

"Waitaminute, you shouldn't be here at all. Aren't I square with Angelica? Her daughter gave me that expensive bike yesterday."

"Ms. Vargas—the mother—would call that a trifle, a simple replacement for the one you lost when saving Dominique. Besides, Dominique bought it for you. My contract with Ms. Vargas, to kill whomever you wish, is her gift to you. That will settle the debt she owes you."

I stood there speechless.

"Welp, I'll get to it, then," Oliver said. "Have a nice life. You won't see me again."

My brain finally started working. "No! Don't kill the guy who stole my bike!"

Oliver looked at me coldly. "Excuse me? You just screamed you wanted him dead. So consider it done, Bernie."

"No! I said that in the heat of the moment! I take it back! Do not kill that man. Give me his name and I'll tell the police."

"I don't work that way, Bernie. Besides, they'll soon be back on the streets after they're arrested. My way, they'll never steal again, or at least, their leader won't."

"No! Leave him alone!" With trembling hands, I fished my cell phone out of my jacket pocket. "I'm calling the cops right now. Give me his name, then get the hell out of here."

"I'll take half your advice," Oliver said. When I looked up, he was gone. I called out for him, but only echoes replied.

Dammit!

I called the police. By the time they arrived, other cycle commuters had come into the basement; some to find their bikes had likewise gone AWOL.

We all gave statements to the cops, who expressed slim hope that we'd ever see our cycles again.

"But, you never know," said one officer, trying to be upbeat.

Yeah, right.

I called for an Uber, which took me into work.

Everyone said they were glad to see me when I walked into my department. "Our very own celebrity," was a common phrase. Some people asked if I had met the girl's father, the notorious Kingpin, and what had I been given in return for saving his daughter's life.

"No, I did not meet the girl's father," I replied, and said nothing else.

My boss barely glanced at me as he rapidly walked by, en route to his corner office, where he'd try to hide out all day. *Jerk.*

Later, on my morning break, I went into our network's research department, one floor up from Master Control where I worked. There was a really nice woman, Emma, who worked there. I'd been trying to ask her out to dinner for months, striking out each time.

"Oh, hey," she said, flashing a warm smile. "Glad you're feeling better. I was worried about you; that was quite a crash. And I like your new clothes. You look really sharp today."

"Thank you," I said, then resolved to get right to the point (I only had a short break). "Can I take you out for dinner tonight, so you can be seen with a sharp-dressed man?"

"Oh, I simply can't, Bernard," Emma said, frowning. "I'm drowning in work. I have to work late almost every night. Sorry."

Another strike-out.

"That's okay," I said, stifling a sigh. "So what're you

working on now?

"Several current stories that need fact-checking before the six o'clock news. That's usual. But it's this other thing I'm digging into. It's for a special report that's scheduled to air in three weeks. A big corporate scandal that's being hushed up. I'm finding hints of some disturbing stuff ..."

Her phone rang, and she started answering the rapid-fire questions of one of our news editors. I quietly left.

Twenty minutes after my shift ended for the day, when Anthony, my replacement, finally showed up (new parent), I left the building and went into a pub down the block for some comfort food. I was alone; my co-workers had families or Significant Others to get home to.

The pub was one of those with multiple screens hanging from the walls and ceiling in strategic locations. Great if you're watching a sports game; intrusive if you're trying to eat in peace.

The evening news came on and I couldn't avoid looking at it. After the usual lead items of war, bloodshed, corruption and political bafflegab, there was a local item that made me choke on my homemade baked lasagna with extra cheese.

"An anonymous tip led police to a small warehouse early this afternoon, where they recovered about a dozen expensive bicycles, that had been reported stolen only this morning," the news anchor read into the cameras. "Here is Lt. Watkins with more details:

"The officers also found several men in an unconscious state in proximity to the stolen goods," intoned the somber-looking lieutenant. "They were a group of men known to us, all with records of theft and assault. They had all been badly beaten. Their leader, in particular, was beaten to within an inch of his life. It was touch and go once we got him to hospital, but doctors now say he is expected to recover. Our investigation continues."

I gawped at the TV, my dinner forgotten.

Oliver?

Chapter Seven:
The Termination

Several days later, I was solidly back into my usual routine. I had retrieved my stolen bike from the police, and had almost worked my way back up to my former brisk pace when cycling to work. Most of my aches and pains had gone.

Detective Kate Millard called me at work, asking how I was and if I had any more details to add about the attempted kidnapping. I said I had already told her everything I knew.

"Well, you're now the last witness to the abduction, besides Dominique herself," Kate said.

"What about the thug I ran into?" I asked. "Is he still in a coma?"

"He's gone."

"Gone? You mean he died?" Nausea flooded me. *Am I now a murderer?*

"No, I mean he's no longer in our custody. Though he was still in a coma, he was handcuffed to the hospital bed, with an officer posted outside his door. When a nurse went in to check on him this morning, all she found was a dangling handcuff."

"How could he just disappear like that?"

"That's what I'd very much like to know, Mr. Keiler. Anyway, that's my problem, not yours. Ride safe and have yourself a nice day."

As the call disconnected, my brain whirled. *Was Angelica behind this? I'm sure she'd love to get her hands on one of the guys who tried to snatch her only child. Or was this the foreign outfit she spoke of, who allegedly hired the kidnappers, anxious to get their man back before he could be questioned?*

Around noon, my boss, the Evil Dictator, stopped by my work station and asked me to see him in his office when my shift ended that afternoon. He bustled off without giving me a chance to ask why.

It was never a good sign to be asked to see the ED in his office. It wasn't time for my annual performance review, so something else must be up. The ED usually didn't bother interacting with us lowly minions.

I spent a nervous afternoon.

Just before my quitting time, Emma from Research came to my station.

"I need a favour, Bernard," she said, frowning, speaking low. "Here, take this and keep it safe."

She handed me a memory stick.

"What's on it?" I asked.

"Something highly confidential. Don't tell anyone you have it. Keep it off site at your home. And don't read what's on it. Okay?"

"Sure, okay, no problem. Hey, maybe you can tell me all about it over dinner?"

She gave a thin smile. "I'm still very busy. But I appreciate having you as a friend."

Emma left and I shoved the stick deep in my jeans pocket. I was finally getting the message she only wanted me as a work colleague, nothing more.

Five minutes after my shift ended, I was in the ED's office. He had lovely views from his windows, as opposed to my windowless room. A bookshelf held his several awards *(achieved on the backs of us minions).*

Looking around his office, you'd never know he ran a sideline business selling real estate—on company time. A clue was that he always carried two cell phones.

The ED was a small weasel of a man, with a middle-aged pot belly and a permanent scowl on his face. His thinning hair was carefully combed to hide his bald spot *(it didn't).* His voice was querulous, and he perspired even on the coldest winter days.

Waving me to a chair, the ED cleared his throat. *Here it comes. He's not one for small talk.*

"Corporate is doing a new round of lay-offs, Bernard,"

he said. "I have to terminate one person in my department. I've narrowed it down to you or Anthony. But Anthony just became a father and his wife is on mat leave."

"So you're saying it's me, even though I'm more qualified than Anthony?" I said, trying to meet his eye. But he avoided looking at me.

"Very possibly, Bernard. You're single with no family responsibilities. But I'll only make my mind up when I return from vacation in two weeks."

"So I get to spend the next two weeks on pins and needles? How kind of you."

The ED bristled. "Well, I did have the courtesy of giving you this heads up. Anthony already knows he's also on the short list; I told him during his lunch hour today."

"Can't you fight this with Corporate?"

"No. Their directive is firm. They must cut costs."

"But the work needs to get done! Who's going to take up the slack after our department is downsized?"

"Corporate has a new computer program which they believe can do many of the routine tasks that each of you do. So fewer personnel should be able to handle the workload."

"But a computer can't fix the technical glitches we regularly get, or handle systems crashes!"

The ED just shrugged. "Higher-ups don't foresee an issue."

I stormed out, before I said something that would get me fired on the spot.

I thought about my union rep, and almost laughed. The union wouldn't back me up beyond lodging a protest. Lay-offs were lay-offs.

About a year ago, our national TV network had been bought by an even-bigger corporation with interests in telecommunications and various media. Predictably, our new owners had started consolidating departments and terminating people across the board, cutting costs wherever they could, all under the guise of "making us more efficient".

I stomped down the stairs leading to the parking lot. Corporate could save money by firing the ED, replacing him with a supervisor at half his inflated salary. The cost savings would allow both Anthony and I to stay employed, with probably enough left to fund the staff Christmas party (one of the first things our new corporate masters had cancelled).

"I hope he dies of a massive heart attack on his damned vacation," I snarled. Then I realized what I'd just said.

"No, I don't want him killed!" I yelled to the deep shadows behind the stairs in the landing.

No voice came from the shadows. Instead, a voice came from halfway down the stairs: "Who are you talking to, Bernard?"

It was Kristen, who worked in Accounting.

"Ah, no one," I replied, flushing red. "I'm...um...rehearsing my lines for a play I'm in."

"Well, you certainly sounded believable," she said.

We both went into the parking lot, she to her car and me to my chained-up bike.

I rode home in a fury.

Two days later, after I'd arrived at work and was settling in at my work station, Anthony rolled in his chair over to me.

"Didja hear?" he asked.

"About what?" I answered. "A snap election's been called? You won the lottery? French fries don't put on weight?"

"No, about our beloved ED. He had a bad accident last night."

A chill went through me. *Oliver again?*

"What happened?" I asked, keeping my voice steady.

"He was showing a house after work—he got a call for a viewing on that special cell phone of his—his wife was home packing for their vacation—they were supposed to leave today—anyway, he slipped on a loose tile at the head of a long staircase leading from a raised back deck to the lawn—and fell all the way down the stairs—he broke his neck!—and one leg—and got a major concussion—he'll be in hospital for weeks—and convalescing at home for months—off on long-term disability."

I gawped at Anthony as he paused for breath. "Then ... then this means he won't be here to fire one of us," I said finally.

"Yeppir!"

"Unless Corporate sends in a new manager."

"Are you kidding?" Anthony snorted. "Not this corporation. They'll leave the position empty, assuming we can fend for ourselves. Which we can. As long as you're here to help me when I get stuck."

Thoughts flooded my brain as I started my daily routine. *Sheer coincidence that the ED slipped on a loose tile? Or had Oliver somehow arranged it? If so, was the accident supposed to have been fatal?*

Chapter Eight:
The Bully

Three days later, I treated myself to dinner at my favourite pub, located about five blocks from my apartment. It was their all-you-can-eat wing night, and they made great lemon-pepper-rub wings.

I was sitting at a round table for four in a corner of the pub, refusing to watch one of their many TVs (I get enough of that at work). I had just ordered a brew and a pile of wings, when three strange, scruffy guys unceremoniously plopped themselves down at my table.

"Hiya, Bernie," said one, a pot-bellied hulking man sporting a massive unkempt beard.

"I'm sorry, but I don't know you folks. You must have the wrong table."

"Aw, ya don't recognize me? It's only been 10 years since high school. 'Course I didn't sport this magnificent beard then. But I'm sure you remember Big Tom from high school, Bernie."

The memory clicked. *Big Tom! The meanest bully in my high school!* He made life a living hell for many kids, and I had been one of them.

"Yeah. I remember you now. How's it going, Tom?"

"Couldn't be better, now that I've found you. I seen you on TV—you're a big shot hero now, eh? This is our first time in this pub—we've been banned from so many others that it's hard to find a place where we're welcome."

"I don't know your two companions."

"Oh, Sid here an' I have been pals since I started working at the airport nine years ago. We're baggage handlers. Rod just got out of prison; he beat some dweeb so bad he almost died. He's now a baggage handler too."

"Nice ... nice to meet you both," I said, hoping my voice was firm.

"Well, we're all awful glad to bump into you, Bernie. Especially since you'll be buying us dinner an' drinks, you bein' such a famous hero an' all."

"Wh...what?"

"Absolutely! An' we're starvin'!" Big Tom gave a piercing whistle, which definitely got the waitress' attention, and bellowed for three beers "toot suite!"

"Look, Tom, I never agreed to buy the three of you dinner or beers."

Tom leaned forward and grabbed my shirt, pulling me forward. "Yes. You. Did. Remember the good times we had in high school? I bet ya still have that scar on your shoulder that I gave ya." *(I did.)*

"Let go!" I slapped his meaty hand away and sat back.

"Your days of bullying me are long past. Now please leave my table."

"We like it here just fine, Bernie. Don't piss us off. You won't like it if we get pissed off."

Abruptly, I stood up. "Gotta visit the can," I said.

As I walked away, one of Tom's cronies said: "Haw! Way ta go, Tom! Scared the wimp so much, he's prolly peed his pants!"

I did not go to the bathroom. I went to the bar, where I knew George, the bartender. I told him those three guys at my table were not wanted there and they refused to leave when I'd asked them to.

"Oh really?" growled George. He was a big, stocky man—six feet tall—and he used to box professionally. Great assets to bounce rowdy patrons. "I'll handle it, Bernard. Stay here."

George grabbed a baseball bat from behind the bar and lumbered over to my table. Towering over the three interlopers, he demanded they leave his bar. Now. Big Tom started to bluster—pointing out there was three of them to one of him—when George pointed out that he had "Priscilla", his persuader, with him, and tapped the bat slowly against his leg.

Tom and George stared hard at each other. Tom saw real menace in George's eyes, like his opponents had in the boxing ring. Tom cursed and rose.

"C'mon, guys," he snarled. "Let's find somewhere nicer to eat."

As they were exiting the doors, Tom yelled back to me: "This ain't over, Bernie, ya wuss!"

"Thanks, George," I said as the bartender returned.

"No prob, Bernard. But watch your back with those assholes. They're trouble."

Excitement over, my beer (just one mug, thankfully) and wings arrived and I had a tasty dinner.

About an hour later, I left the pub, after thanking George again for removing my unwanted guests. I looked up and down the sidewalk and street. No sign of Big Tom and his goons. I sighed in relief.

I walked around the corner of the pub, to the bike rack. There was a paved side alley next to the rack. On the other side of the alley was one of Toronto's wooded ravines.

.   I stopped. Standing in front of the bike rack, which only had one bike chained to it (mine), were Big Tom and his goons.

"Hiya, Bernie," Tom rumbled. "Figgered this was your bike; I saw your sissy helmet hanging from the back of your chair."

"Clear off, you guys," I commanded in a forceful tone. "Leave me alone. I don't want any trouble."

"Oh, too late for that, Bernie. Y'see, we do want trouble. It was very rude of ya to have us thrown outta that pub. All we wanted was a peaceable dinner."

"Yeah, a dinner you were forcing me to buy for you."

"Forcing? Here I thought you were doing it 'cause you're a nice guy."

I marched up to the trio. "Yes, forcing. Now get away from my bike."

Tom moved faster than his bulk suggested. I suddenly found myself hard against the wall of the pub with a very big knife pointing at my chest.

"Shut up, wuss. I'm in control here, just like in high school. Now you're gonna stay put an' look while my buds tear apart that pretty bike of yours. Looks expensive."

I watched, horrified, as Sid and Rod went to my bike. They each pulled out short crow bars from their back pockets.

One of them—Rod?—lifted his crowbar over the bike's carbon-fibre frame. Then he gave an "Urk" sound and collasped onto the pavement.

"What th' hell?" said the other. "Hey, Tom, looks like a big rock hit him. Whaddya think hap - "

The thug suddenly said "Urk" himself and followed his mate to the ground.

Big Tom's head whipped around. "What the fu -"

Then I did something I've never done in my life.

My left arm swatted Tom's knife hand away. At the same time, I punched him—hard—right where I figured his chin to be under his bushy beard. *It worked! Just like on TV!*

There was a satisfying *smack!* The bully's head snapped back and he fell backward like a felled tree, crashing to the pavement. I was astonished to see he was out cold.

I'll be damned! Big Tom the bully, terror of my high school, had a glass jaw!

I called 911 and reported anonymously I had just incapacitated three muggers, and gave this location. I disconnected, unchained my bike, and pedaled furiously for home.

I was still full of adrenalin, so pleased with myself that I had clocked the bully who had terrified me in high school, that I forgot to question who had been hidden in the woods where the rocks had come from.

Chapter Nine:
The Dinner

Two days later, to my surprise, I received a text from Dominique. With her mother's resources, I'm sure it was easy getting my cell phone number. After all, she'd found my apartment address to deliver the bike.

"How is tomorrow night for that dinner I promised you?" the text read.

"Great. I'm free." *Huh. She was actually serious about having dinner with me! I can't even get Emma to have dinner with me.*

"Perfect. I'll pick you up at 7 outside your front lobby. Dress nice. Oh, this is my treat."

"Can I at least buy the wine?"

"K."

Turned out our dinner *(date?)* was at one of the city's finest restaurants; regular people had to reserve six months ahead to get a table—the length of time they'd probably need in order to save up to afford it.

Thomas picked me up right on time. Dominique was already in the car. She did not look like a university student tonight. She had transformed into an absolutely stunning woman, wearing a figure-hugging royal blue designer dress with matching shoes and clutch purse. Her dress was slit high to her upper thigh on one side, revealing a muscular leg. She wore sparkling jewelry, which I'm sure wasn't fake. Her long auburn hair was beautifully styled.

For myself, I wore my best suit; the one her mother had bought me at that upscale men's shop. It was the only suit I owned that still had all its buttons.

"Wow. You look great," I said.

"Thanks. You look pretty sharp yourself," she smiled.

"Hey, thanks for taking me out."

She grinned. "My pleasure. I don't often get to dress up like this, y'know."

As the maitre d' led us to our table, Dominique walked ahead of me. Her sleek dress had an open back almost down to her waist. There was no bra strap.

After we were seated, I perused the wine list. And almost choked. The prices were in the stratosphere. I finally selected a bottle that would only cost me a week's salary. (Wine by the glass was not available; too gauche, I suspected.)

Then we looked at the menu. Again, I almost choked. The appetizers alone cost what an entire dinner cost at my favorite roadhouse restaurant.

"Are ... are you sure you want to pay for dinner?" I asked.

She laughed. "Don't worry. I have a generous trust fund. So order whatever you like, okay?"

I looked for something cheap, but they didn't have burgers, or even mac and cheese. The waiter suggested tonight's chef special—a duck confection—and, in desperation, I ordered that. Dominique ordered venison medallions in a special wine sauce.

After we ordered, she leaned forward, staring at me. I made a point of looking at her perfectly made-up face, not at the top of her low-cut dress, which showed significant cleavage.

"Can I call you Bernie?" she asked.

Though I hated being called Bernie, I nodded. *I could drown in her blue eyes.*

"Bernie, I like total honesty, so let's promise to answer questions truthfully, okay?"

I nodded again. I loved the way her mouth quirked up at the corners when she talked.

She asked what I did, and I explained my job at the TV network.

"Sounds interesting. How'd you get that job?"

"I have a degree in Television Broadcasting from Mohawk College in Hamilton. I was at the top of my class; in fact, I got hired by my network before I'd even graduated. But I still had to graduate—they wanted that degree—

so I worked part-time with them until graduation. The downside is that I'm in a highly-specialized field. I can do a lot in the world of TV Master Control, but not much outside that world. So it's worrisome when our new corporate boss starts downsizing."

"Yeah, I can see that." Then she asked about my hobbies.

"Well, you already know I'm an avid cyclist—thanks again for my new bike, by the way. It's really awesome. My other hobby is, ah, somewhat unusual."

Her eyebrows rose. "Well? Give."

"Um, well, don't laugh, but I collect old, rare superhero comic books. It's a challenge finding them in good quality at a price I can afford."

"Old superhero comics? You mean like Batman, Spider-Man, Hulk, Superman, like that? Like in the movies?"

"Yeah. Especially comics from the 1960s and 70s. Though they originally only cost 12 or 15 cents back then, they're worth hundreds and sometimes thousands of dollars now. Key issues, with a popular character's first appearance, are especially valuable."

"So what's your most valuable comic?"

I thought a moment. *"Incredible Hulk #181,* the first appearance of Wolverine. It's graded Near Mint and currently worth over $16,000. More if you sell it on eBay. I keep it in a safety deposit box at my bank."

Dominique's eyebrows shot up and she shook her head. "Wow."

"Oh, some comics are worth far more. The two most famous ones are the first appearances of Superman and Spider-Man. They sold at auction for over three million each in Near Mint condition. It's very rare to find them in that condition."

"So comics are a good investment?"

"Oh yeah, but you have to buy carefully and ensure they're accurately graded."

"Well, you weren't kidding—you certainly do have an unusual hobby. What are you, 35?"

"I'm 28," I bristled. "And I know from the news that you're 23."

"Guilty as charged, Bernie. Um, do you have a significant other?"

"I had a girlfriend, but we broke up amicably seven months ago. Just weren't right for each other. Nothing serious since then. How about you?"

"Like you, nothing serious. About a year ago, Mother tried to hook me up with a British aristocrat—a duke or earl or somesuch—but after one date, I ghosted him. So full of himself, everything had to be all about him."

I asked about school and hobbies.

"I don't have a lot of time for hobbies. I'm a full-time grad student, taking a Masters of Business Administration at the University of Toronto's Rotman School of Management. U of T is where I earned my Bachelor of Commerce. When I'm not studying, I'm on the varsity track and field team. I love downhill skiing and SCUBA diving. And I like to cycle, like you."

"An MBA? Good for you. That's a challenging course of study."

"It's all so I can be an asset to the family businesses," she said.

"Ah, your family businesses," I said, suddenly nervous. "You're, um, okay with that?"

I felt a chill descend between us. "Don't believe what the news media tells you. My mother runs several highly-profitable legitimate businesses. But because she's a woman succeeding in a man's world, people trash-talk her. It's very hurtful."

Those were almost exactly the words her mother had said to me. Is that their pat answer to outsiders? Or does Dominique really not know about her mother's criminal activities?

Aloud I said: "I apologize. Sorry I brought it up."

I changed the topic to trips we had taken. I had traveled more than most people, but always at sale prices. Dominique was also well-traveled: by private jet to exclusive resorts, or her family's villas in the Swiss Alps and

St. Barts.

"Wow, you certainly move in different circles than me," I said.

"Maybe, but I'm still human too," she smiled. "And I'm enjoying this dinner with you, Bernie."

"Oh, likewise for me. You're wonderful company. So, um, are your new bodyguards here?" I asked.

"Oh yes, a husband-wife team, but they're quite discreet. You'll notice them only if I get up to use the Ladies; Bethany will follow me inside."

I looked around the restaurant—I couldn't help myself —trying to spot the bodyguards, looking for a couple trying to fit in where they did not. Then I stopped and returned my attention to Dominique. *Why look around when you've got this beautiful vision right in front of you, all to yourself, stupidhead?*

The rest of the dinner went very well. The service was snobbishly slow, but it gave us lots of time to talk. The way-overpriced food was excellent. She approved of my wine selection, though I had to admit to myself that it tasted about the same as my $15 bottle of plonk that I had at home.

After dessert, as we awaited our coffees (hers was an Italian concoction I'd never heard of), she excused herself to visit the bathroom. I watched her shimmy around the tables and disappear down the corridor to the washrooms. I noticed I wasn't the only set of male eyes ogling her. *Those guys must be jealous that a twit like me is out with such a stunning woman.*

It hit me several minutes later. *Hey, waitaminute. Wasn't her female bodyguard supposed to follow her into the Ladies?*

No one had followed her.

Chapter Ten:
The Dance

I jerked upright and scanned the room, wanting to give her bodyguards hell because Dominique had left while they were asleep on the job. Then I realized I had no idea what they looked like.

I quickly walked through the dining room to the corridor leading to the washrooms. It was a long corridor with subdued lighting. As I approached the end, I saw something was wrong.

What happened next was like watching an elaborately-choreographed dance, in slow motion. Though in hindsight, it happened very fast.

I first saw blobs of black and flashes of blue. It resolved itself into two big black shapes holding a struggling Dominique. *This is déjà vu!* One black shape had its hand clamped over her mouth. I started running towards them.

"Let her go!" I shouted.

One black shape released her and turned toward me. The other—the one blocking her mouth—kept a firm grip on Dominique.

Suddenly, with a guttural cry, she wrenched herself free of her captor, tearing the top of her lovely dress as she did so. Turning to face him, she snarled:

"I REFUSE to be made a victim a second time!"

Then she kicked him hard between his legs, driving her pointed shoe deep into his personals. The thug screamed and dropped to his knees, doubled over. He retched.

The man facing me turned and tried to grab Dominique again. She danced backward and aimed a kick at his crotch. He evaded it and savagely backhanded her into the wall. She hit with a sickening thud and crumpled to the floor.

That's when I hit him with an expert martial arts move that knocked him flat.

No, not really.

When I was almost on him, I slipped on something hard and round. I promptly lost my balance, twisted, and hit the wall at full speed.

With the grace of a ballet dancer, I bounced off the wall and into the thug, sending us both crashing to the ground.

The man swore and twisted around, pinning me to the floor. His large rough hands found my throat and started squeezing. Taking my cue from Dominique, I tried to knee him in the privates, but he had my legs pinned.

I fought his grip around my throat, but it was like a fly attacking a gorilla. Bright dots of colours appeared in my vision and my lungs informed me that they could really use a breath, please.

I started blacking out.

There was a sharp *thwack* and the gorilla's face went slack. He grunted, fell over, and lay still. Still half-pinned under his bulk, barely-conscious, I lay gasping for air, sweet beautiful air.

A cold voice whispered in my ear: "You're welcome."

Then Dominique was there, one hand clutching the top of her torn dress closed and the other helping move the thug off me. Then we both sat down side-by-side, panting, our backs against the wall. I saw she was shaking.

I took off my jacket. "Here, put this on and button it. It'll warm you and save you from embarrassment."

She shrugged into the garment. "Thanks Bernie. And thanks for saving me again. I hope you didn't see anything, um, immodest."

"Not at all," I lied. *She didn't need more embarrassment.* "And I didn't so much as save you from the second man, as I offered my neck to be strangled instead."

People had heard the commotion and someone had called 911. I put my arm around her while we waited for the cops. She was still shaking.

"I'm so mad," she gritted in a low voice. "Once again, I've been made into a cliché: damsel in distress—this time even with a torn dress—saved by a man from a fate worse than death. Aargh!"

"Um, it was two against one, Dominique," I said. "And you incapacitated one of them by yourself."

"Yeah, that was satisfying."

"And you did more than that: you saved me by knocking out the thug who was strangling me."

"I didn't do that. When I came to, I saw him lying atop you, out cold, with you trying to get him off you. I assumed you had hit him."

She leaned her head on my shoulder. *Mmm, her shampoo smells very nice.*

"Whatever," she murmured. "It seems you're my very own personal superhero. I'll have to get you a colourful costume."

I chuckled. "I'll also need a dramatic name, like Captain Klutz, and a catchy battle cry, like 'It's clobberin' time!', though that one's already taken. Oh, and I own the movie and TV rights."

Paramedics bustled in, led to us by the maitre d' who apologized profusely, saying he was absolutely mortified that such an incident happened at his restaurant.

The medics shooed him away, then examined us. We were both in fair shape. I'd have lovely bruises around my neck and on my right shoulder where I'd slammed into the wall. Besides a bloody lip, Dominique had been gifted with bruises on her upper arms, where the kidnappers had held her, and on her forehead where she'd hit the wall after being backhanded. The paramedics wanted to take her to the hospital so a doctor could assess her and for an MRI head scan, since she had been knocked unconscious, but she refused.

"I have a hard head," she said.

The police finally arrived and took our statements. The thug who'd throttled me was carted off, still unconscious. The other thug, the one Dominique had kicked in the balls, was nowhere to be seen. We figured he'd recovered and slipped out the back door leading off the corridor, which the cops said is how the kidnappers got in. Then they had waited in an alcove for Dominique to visit the restroom.

The back door led to an alley, where the goons had their vehicle parked. The escaped goon had taken it.

The cops found a glass jar on the floor, half-full of chloroform. That was what I had slipped on. The kidnappers had obviously planned to drug Dominique with the chloroform, but because she struggled so much, they hadn't yet been able to do it before I showed up.

We wondered what had happened to Dominique's two bodyguards. It was only the next day when we got our answer. Their bodies were discovered in a dumpster in the alley. Somehow, they had both been lured out there.

When the cops were done, Dominique fished out her cellphone from her purse and made a call. Then she stood, announcing, "Now I really have to use the bathroom," and scooted inside.

When she emerged, Thomas was there with four burly men who looked like they hadn't smiled since they were babies. After making sure Dominique was all right, Thomas turned to me and shook my hand.

"Thank you for saving our special lady again, Mr. Keiler," he said.

"Oh, she mostly saved herself this time," I replied, smiling.

Thomas and the four men surrounded Dominique and led her outside to the waiting Lincoln. Two of the men got into the town car, the other two clambered into a black SUV parked right behind.

Before getting in the car, Dominique turned and said: "Well, take care of yourself, Comic Book Guy." *Ah, a* Simpsons *fan.*

"You too, MBA Gal," I replied. "Thanks for dinner."

She laughed wryly, got in and Thomas closed the door.

I watched as they drove off, leaving me standing alone. I suddenly realized my wallet was in my jacket pocket, and Dominique was still wearing my jacket.

I was able to convince a cop to drive me home in his squad car. As I got out of the car, old Mrs. Dumfries from my building was doing a late-night walk of her usually ill-tempered dog. She looked at me and sniffed.

"In trouble with the law again, eh, Mr. Keiler?" she said.

"Mrs. Dumfries, I have never been in trouble with the law," I retorted.

"Hogwash. I recall seeing you on the news recently."

"Yeah, because I had just saved a young woman from being kidnapped!"

"Fake news," she proclaimed and walked off.

As I was drifting off to sleep, after taking two extra-strength Tylenols, I had a sudden thought: *Had someone said "you're welcome" in my ear? Or had I imagined it, in my semi-conscious state?*

Chapter Eleven:
The Confrontation

I was expecting the call, and it came two days later.

"May I pick you up in an hour, Mr. Keiler?" asked Thomas.

"Do I have a choice?" I said.

"No."

The line went dead. Luckily, it was my day off. *Maybe luck had nothing to do with it; they probably knew my shift schedule at work.*

The day before, Detective Millard had called me, asking for more details about the second attempted kidnapping. She had already spoken to Dominique. I had nothing new to add to the statement I had already provided.

I knew there would be another call, and not from the police.

An hour later, as I slid onto the leather back seat of the Lincoln, Thomas handed me a thick package wrapped in brown paper. "Your jacket, Sir, dry cleaned and pressed. And here's your wallet."

I thanked him for both items, shoving my wallet into my jeans pocket.

About 50 minutes later, I was ushered into Angelica Vargas' imposing office. This time, she got up from behind her desk and came around it to shake my hand. She wore a navy blue business suit today, which of course fitted perfectly.

"Bernard, so good to see you again," she said, smiling. I was reminded of Bruce, the smiling shark from *Finding Nemo*.

"Um, good to see you too Ms. Var ... I mean, Angelica."

She indicated a chair across from her desk and she resumed her seat behind the desk.

"It seems I am once again in your debt, Bernard. Thank you for again saving Dominique. Perhaps I should hire you as her bodyguard."

I chuckled. "No thanks. Her bodyguards have a short life span, from what I've seen."

She inclined her head.

"I'm happy to have helped," I continued, "but as I told Thomas two days ago, this time she did most of the saving herself. And forget that debt business please; your thanks is all I need."

Angelica regarded me steadily, unblinking. "Indeed. However, this is an obligation I still feel strongly about."

"Please don't. As I said during my last visit, I'm just happy I was able to be of assistance. How's Dominique doing?"

"Physically, she is on the mend. Mentally, she is understandably quite upset at being the target of two attempted kidnappings. I have sent her to our cottage in Northern Ontario to recuperate. It is very secluded; accessible only by float plane. Only a select few know of its existence, much less its location."

"A wise decision. So what steps are you taking to stop these kidnapping attempts?"

She stared at me for a long time. *Have I overstepped my bounds? Remember who you're talking to!*

"I normally do not disclose my plans to outsiders, Bernard," she said. "But you have proven your worth twice now, so I will answer you. I have discovered the person in the rival family who ordered the kidnappings. But I am in a quandary. The attacks on my daughter cannot go unanswered. But an assassination will likely lead to our two families going to war. That would be bad for business. Bad for innocents."

"Why not just give the name of the person responsible to the cops? I talked with Detective Millard yesterday, and they are no closer to solving the case than they were after the first attempt to take Dominique."

"The police will require evidence, proof. I do not have that. But I am convinced my information is accurate. I paid enough for it."

"Oh."

"Now back to our business. I understand you have so far refused my gift of Oliver's services."

"Thanks for bringing that up. Yeah. There's no way I want his services. Forgive my directness, but it was rude of you to think I would use a professional assassin. I told you before, no gift is necessary. I don't consider you to have a debt with me."

"And as I previously made clear to you, I do not see it that way. You have done me a great service—twice now."

I groaned in exasperation. "Look, Dominique just took me out to a fine dinner. We had an enjoyable evening—well, up until the kidnapping attempt. So I think you and I are even, because you let me have dinner with your daughter."

"Oh, I do not 'let' Dominique do anything, Bernard. She is a grown woman now and does what she wishes."

After an uncomfortable silence, Angelica said: "There is another reason I asked you here today. We have other business to deal with. Oliver has asked to see me and he seems upset. I thought it best if you were here too."

She picked up her desk phone and said: "Send in Oliver."

Seconds later, the man in black strode in. He scowled when he saw me. I scowled right back.

Angelica indicated the other chair and Oliver deposited his tall lean frame into it.

"I understand you are upset about something," she said.

"Yeah, and he's sittin' right beside me. Ms. Vargas, you assigned me to Bernie here, to snuff anyone he wished, no questions asked. Problem is: he doesn't want me to kill anyone! It's been almost a month, an' I haven't killed anyone! I'm gettin' real frustrated!"

Oliver glared at me. I glared back.

"But you are being handsomely compensated for your time, Oliver," Angelica said.

"Yeah, thank you, but that ain't the point! I'm hired to kill people. That's what I do. But I haven't been allowed to kill anyone with this job! Since I turned pro, I've never gone this long without killin' someone! If somethin' doesn't happen soon, I'm gonna haveta start charging you for therapy sessions!"

"It would be unseemly of me to take back a gift," she said, then looked at me. "It is a matter of honour."

"Look, your money hasn't been completely wasted, Ms. Vargas," Oliver said. "I've been shadowing Bernie, keepin' close tabs on him, hopin' that he'll point me at a target, so I can fulfill my contract with you. But so far he hasn't given me a target. It's drivin' me nuts!"

"Hold on," I broke in. "So it was you responsible for my mysterious rescues? The gang that stole my new bike, my boss taking a bad fall, the rocks thrown at those bullies, and knocking out the gorilla strangling me?"

"Yup. I figgered I had to keep you alive an' happy until you finally told me who you wanted killed. So I've been your lethal shadow, Bernie. I saved your life with that strangler."

"Yes, I realize that. Thank you, Oliver."

"Welcome. But I'm proudest of the almost-lethal accident I staged for your boss. I arranged the house showing. I knew he'd lead the prospective buyers out to the backyard—the buyers were friends of mine who I'd told to ask to see it—so I loosened the top tile of the staircase, figuring he'd slip on it. Took care of your imminent job termination problem, eh?"

"Yeah, but - "

"May I say, Bernie boy, that you have been uncommonly unlucky this past month. You've been in one bad situation after another. Is your life always like this?"

"No," I said. "I'm usually the quiet little mouse that no one notices."

"Let us focus on our problem here," interjected Angelica. "Bernard refuses to accept my gift and Oliver is exceedingly frustrated at not being able to relieve anyone of their life."

"Pardon me for wantin' to do my job," Oliver groused.

I suddenly had an inspiration. "I have a suggestion that will solve all three of our problems, including the asshole trying to kidnap Dominique. Give the job to Oliver! He says he's the best and he specializes in making it look like an accident. I didn't ask for an assassin to be assigned to me, and I refuse to use him. So simply reassign him to avenging Dominique's two attempted kidnappings. Have him kill the guy responsible and make it look like an accident. Then there'd be no gang war. It's an elegant solution!"

"Interesting," Angelica said. "What say you, Oliver?"

"Don't matter to me, Ms. Vargas. I just wanna kill someone."

"Are you absolutely sure you wish to give up this gift, Bernard?"

I nodded. "Absolutely."

"Then it is done. Oliver, I hereby reassign you to terminate the scum who ordered Dominique's abductions. I shall give you full details tomorrow. He is very hard to get to."

Oliver beamed. "Good. I love a challenge. I'm very hard to keep out, as Bernie knows."

I rose. "Thank you for being so reasonable, Angelica. Gook luck, Oliver."

Angelica nodded. Oliver grinned: "Thanks, but I don't need luck."

The assassin stood, fished in a pocket, and brought out a slim device with a red button on it.

"In spite of everything, I've taken a shine to you these past weeks, Bernie boy. You need a guardian angel at times. So here, take this. It works like a pager. It sends a signal via satellite to my receiver anywhere in the world. You ever need me, I'll come. Free of charge. But only once."

As I started to refuse, Oliver pressed it into my hand. "I insist."

I made my goodbyes. *This will be the last time I see either of you,* I vowed. Thomas drove me home.

Back in my apartment, I tore open the thick parcel Thomas had given me earlier. I gasped. Beneath my cleaned and pressed suit jacket, was another new suit! Different in colour and design from the first suit, it likewise was exquisitely tailored.

There was a card from the exclusive men's store that had measured me and furnished the first suit, with a message in Dominique's well-formed handwriting:

"You look so good in the first suit, so I thought you could use a second one." Beneath the message was an elegant "D".

Now what do I read into this?

Chapter Twelve
The Secret

I awoke in the middle of the night and couldn't get back to sleep. My brain was in turmoil.

Had I once again been a hypocrite? Not about accepting the second bespoke suit—it was Dominique's gift after all— but being so nonplussed about freeing Oliver to terminate the guy behind her kidnapping attempts, after preaching about not wanting Oliver to kill anyone of my choosing.

So it was okay for him to kill someone of Angelica's choosing, but not mine? Was my conscience clear? Did I have selective morals?

Dawn found me shambling morosely around my apartment in my bespoke ratty PJs, doing laundry, putting things away, having cereal for breakfast with milk that had only expired a week ago. The glorious life of a bachelor.

I realized today was garbage day. As I was about to tie the trash bag closed, I remembered the hi-tech paging device Oliver had given me. I fished it out of my pants pocket and dropped it into the bag, tying it shut and carrying it out.

I don't want any part of that world. Nope. No way I'd ever summon Oliver anyway.

After I'd arrived at work and poured myself a cup of

the tepid sewer sludge that passed as coffee, Anthony wheeled in his chair over to my work station.

"Didja hear?" he asked.

"About what?" I answered. "Trudeau's resigned and joined a hippie commune? Alberta separated from Canada and Quebec's furious because they hadn't done it first? The Toronto Maple Leafs finally won the Stanley Cup for the first time since 1967?"

He rolled his eyes. "No, Emma in Research is missing."

"What?"

"Yeah. She hasn't shown up for work in days, she never contacted Scheduling to request time off, there's no answer by phone or at her apartment. Nada. HR contacted her parents and sister; they've heard nothing either. Her boss is furious."

"Wow, that totally doesn't sound like her. She's a compulsive workaholic."

"Yep, it's a mystery," Anthony said. "Her work area was trashed too, like someone was looking for something. Quite a mess, I hear." He rolled back to his station.

What had happened to Emma? Then 12 of the TV stations in Atlantic Canada under my watch suddenly went black, and I was so busy restoring their feeds that I forgot about Emma. (Our national headquarters in Toronto was responsible for affiliate TV stations from Atlantic Canada to Alberta. Excluding Quebec, of course.)

When the technicians finally arrived, I had restored 10 of the 12 stations. They checked my work, and restored the remaining two stations. Then I had to endure a chewing-out from their union rep for doing work that was clearly under their purview As per our collective agreement, technical issues were to be handled by technicians; us Master Controllers were supposed to sit idle until the almighty techs arrived to work their magic. My Evil Dictator boss, had he been there, would also have happily chewed me out.

You're welcome and screw you.

Back home after a long day, I was deciding which frozen alien meal to microwave for dinner, when my cell phone rang.

"Yell-o," I said.

"Bernard? It's Emma."

"Emma! You okay? You sound like you've been crying. Where are you? Everyone's wondering what happened to you. What's going on?"

"Yes, I've been crying," she said, sniffing. "And I can't tell you where I am. My research got noticed; it set off somebody's alarm. I started getting threatening phone calls, telling me to stop digging, to drop the story. People were following me, and my apartment was broken into and ransacked. They're looking for the stick."

"The stick?"

"Yes, that memory stick I gave you. You still have it?"

"Of course. But what's so damn important about that stick?"

"You haven't read what's on it?"

"No. I promised you I wouldn't."

"Good. Then you're safe. Don't tell anyone you have it. That's very important. The people after me are very nasty; you don't want them coming at you."

"So what are you doing now?"

There was a long pause. Then Emma said: "Three days ago, a guy tried to follow me into my apartment, but I slammed the door in his face. That was the last straw. The next day, my wife and I left on the first flight we could get. We're in Australia now, visiting her relatives in the Outback. We're completely off the grid—I'm even calling you on a satellite-uplink phone. The scumbags will never find us here."

Wife? Well, she certainly kept that secret. That explained why I could never get a date with her.

"But listen, Bernard," Emma continued. "If you don't hear from me in a week, give that stick to Ralph or Betty in News (they were senior news editors). Tell them it's explosive stuff, from me."

"Whaddya mean, explosive stuff?"

"You remember I was working on a special project, digging deep into some corporate funny business? Not our new corporate owners; I mean a huge multi-national conglomerate."

"Yeah. So what did you dig up?"

"Something that would rock the business world, and our federal government, to the core. Something worth killing for, to keep it secret. For your own sake, that's all I can tell you."

"Why not just give it to Ralph or Betty now, to blow the whistle on it? That would take the heat off you."

"Because my work isn't finished yet. The case isn't airtight yet; those responsible could still wiggle out of it, denying everything. That's also why I haven't called the cops. For now, just keep that stick safe, Bernard. And don't open it!"

"Okay, sure, you can count on me, Emma."

"Thanks. You're a wonderful friend." She hung up.

So of course the first thing I did was plug her stick into my laptop and open it.

Reading the material, I must have said "holy shit!" at least six times. Then I read it again. And swore again.

I copied all the material on the stick to a second memory stick, as insurance.

I'd been hiding Emma's stick in my sock drawer *(no one would ever think of looking there, right?)*. But after reading the material, and now knowing "they" were prone to breaking into homes and tossing them, I figured I needed a better hiding place.

How about in plain sight? I had a "junk jar" on a shelf above my desk, full of miscellaneous nuts, bolts, screws, elastic bands, pens, pencils, and a red clown nose *(don't ask)*. I shoved the stick in the bottom of the jar.

Now I had to think of an even-cleverer hiding place for the second stick. Thanks to countless TV shows, I knew that air vents were a favourite hiding place, so therefore that would be what meticulous searchers would check. Ditto things taped to the backs of pictures *(not that I had a lot of pictures on my walls)*. Freezers were also a popular spot to hide guns, drugs, illegal cash, and body parts.

Then I had an inspiration *(yes, I sometimes do get them)*. I placed the stick in a small freezer bag and buried it in the middle of a pound of fresh ground beef (extra lean) that I'd planned to grill up this weekend. I put the beef in a larger freezer bag, and stuffed it at the back of my fridge's freezer. Anyone tossing the freezer would just see a frozen bag of meat.

Then I dressed and cycled to work, in a daze. My head was in a whirl. What was on that stick would definitely shake the stock market, destroy several well-known companies, and likely bring down our federal government.

It could also get Emma—and now me—killed to keep it secret.

I needed some heavy-duty protection. *And what had I just thrown away this morning?*

Chapter Thirteen
The Garbage

The next day, I had an alien visitor from another planet.

It happened at work during a 16-hour double shift (New Dad Anthony had to stay home with his sick baby, because his wife was also very sick).

My unexpected alien visitor was a Suit from the Head Office section of our sprawling building: Martin Bledsoe, Vice-President of Something (one of our network's confusing gaggle of VPs with vague titles). He had a tennis-tanned face with not a hair out of place on his barbered head. His suit was tailored, of the same expensive quality as my two new bespoke suits.

I was astonished. Suits from Head Office *never* visited where the work was actually being done, except if they were touring the Prime Minister or Premier or other high dignitary through our expansive building (where they often got lost). Bledsoe had actually managed to find me in Master Control all by himself.

After a bare modicum of small talk, Bledsoe asked if Emma had spoken with me before her disappearance. I said she'd come down for a quick chat.

"Did she say where she was going?" asked the Suit.

"No. Not even a hint. I had no idea she was going

anywhere."

"Hmm. Did she give you anything?"

"No," I lied. I hoped I was a good liar. *(Turned out later that I wasn't.)*

"Hmm. You're sure?"

"Yes. What was she supposed to have given me?"

"Hmm. Never mind, Bernard. Keep up the good work." Bledsoe left, doubtless proud of his rousing pep talk.

At the company cafeteria that night, deciding what lukewarm toxic waste I wanted to endanger my digestive tract with by eating it, a colleague asked what the Suit had wanted with me. She had seen him talking with me through my section's open door as she went down the corridor.

"Just asked me some questions about Emma," I said. "But I didn't know anything."

"Yeah, it's strange she just disappeared like that. It's even stranger that a Suit is interested."

"Yeah."

"They should file a Missing Persons report, y'know, get the cops looking for her."

"Yeah."

My double shift ended at midnight. I rode home through quiet streets, illuminated by staccato pools of street light. My brain was tired mush, but my body appreciated the exercise and fresh air after 16 hours stuck inside riding a chair.

I brought my bike up the elevator and wheeled it into my apartment (I had taken Oliver's advice).

As I closed my door, the smell hit me.

"Gah! It smells like a damn garbage dump in here!" I said.

"Do tell," a familiar voice said.

I flicked on a light. Sitting on my couch was the man in black. But he was no longer black. His clothes were splattered with a rainbow of colours, some of which looked wet. The strong garbage smell came from him.

"Oliver!" I yelped. "What the hell are you doing here —it's one in the morning—and why do you stink like a dumpster?"

"I'm sitting here deciding whether to kill you, Bernie. Because it's your f**king fault I smell and look this way."

"What the hell are you talking about?"

Oliver held up a small device. "Recognize this?"

"That's ... that's the pager you gave me."

"Correct. The expensive pager that you obviously threw in the garbage."

"Well, yeah, okay I did. So why do you have it?"

Oliver leaned back into the couch. I suddenly realized his filthy clothes were dirtying my formerly-clean light blue couch fabric.

"What do you think happens when you throw something into the trash, Bernie boy?"

"It ... it goes to the city dump."

Oliver sighed. "Lemme tell you somethin' about garbage. Collected garbage first goes to a staging centre at the dump, where it's lumped in with tons of other collected garbage. Then it gets hauled away, either to be compacted for the landfill, or incinerated. At the staging centre, in a big pile of fresh garbage, something pressed against the panic button here, and set it off.

"Now try and keep up with me on this, Bernie. I get the signal and track it to the staging centre. I'm shocked. I figure someone iced you and dumped your body in with thousands of tons of trash. It's been done before; I speak from personal experience. But I have to make sure. So I break into the dump tonight, after they've closed. I dig into the pile of garbage where your signal is coming from. But I don't find your body, Bernie. I find this pager!"

The tall man unfolded from the couch and towered over me. "And how do you think that makes me feel?"

"Um, relieved that I'm still alive?"

"NO."

"Um, a little upset that you went dumpster diving for nothing?"

"YES. I was in the middle of gathering observational intel on my new target—he is indeed hard to get to—when your pager went off. So I drop everything and chase the signal. Only to end up swimmin' in garbage! Did I ever tell you I hate getting dirty?"

"Um, no."

"It's one of my little hang-ups. Besides enjoying killing people."

"Um, sorry about this, Oliver. I didn't mean for this to happen."

"You never even thought to take the battery out before you chucked it! That would have made it just a useless piece of plastic."

"Sorry."

"Y'know, you're really too pathetic to kill. You idiot. But you are paying my cleaning bill for these clothes, and my car interior. *Capiche?*"

I nodded.

As Oliver moved to the door, I blurted: "Hey, um, I may

have need for you to be my lethal protector again. I seem to have gotten myself mixed up in a major corporate mess that some people will kill to keep secret."

He stopped and glared at me. I think I wilted.

"How dare you even ask me, after what you just put me through! You're probably too thick to notice, but I'm really, really pissed at you. It's only by great force of will that I don't shoot you right now."

"I appreciate your self-control. And I said I'm sorry. But I think I might need your special talents to keep me safe."

"You have me confused with a bodyguard, Bernie. I'm an assassin."

"But, but you helped me before," I whined.

"That was a professional courtesy to Ms. Vargas. But you're not my assignment anymore, remember? So my answer is no."

The tall dark man slid past me and opened my door. *(Man, he really stank something fierce!)* As he left, Oliver said in a low tone:

"I warn you. You ever see me again, it'll be the last thing you see."

He left with the pager.

Chapter Fourteen:
The Invasion

Two days after my odorous encounter with Oliver (it had taken me forever to clean my couch the next day), I was doing another 16-hour double shift at my beloved network *(sarcasm)*.

I really didn't mind pulling doubles. Though it was hard on my body, the pay was excellent: regular pay for the first eight hours, time-and-a-half for the next four hours, and double-time for the last four. Plus the company gave me a meal voucher for dinner, though what masqueraded as dinner in our cafeteria should have warranted a bright red "Facility Closed" notice from the Health Inspector.

No one had heard anything new about Emma. (I had, but I kept my mouth shut.)

My double shift ended at midnight. Arriving home just before 1:00 a.m., I gingerly opened my apartment door and sniffed. No nauseating garbage smell. Just a faint scent of the cleaner I'd used on my couch.

I stepped inside with my bike, flipped on a light, closed the door, turned, and was gobsmacked by a disaster.

Everything in sight was overturned, strewn on the floor, broken, or slashed. Air vents had been ripped from the walls. Pictures were down. It looked like a localized hurricane had hit my apartment. In shock, I walked through my kitchen and bedroom - same chaos.

My sanctum had been invaded!

I suddenly realized that the invaders had been looking for the memory stick I was hiding for Emma. None of my valuables had been taken, including my stash of old comic books. The emergency cash in my dresser drawer was untouched, though it and the rest of the contents were all over the floor.

I went to my desk. The "junk jar" had been taken from the shelf and upended on my desk.

Emma's memory stick was gone.

I ran back into the kitchen. Food from both fridge and freezer lay on the floor. I yanked open the freezer door. What was left inside was chaos; they had obviously riffled through the contents. I frantically dug to the back of the freezer.

The bag of ground chuck, with the second stick in its centre, was still there.

Relieved, I restocked fridge and freezer with the displaced items, then called the police to report the home invasion. I would need their report to file an insurance claim for the damaged stuff, like my freshly-cleaned couch and my mattress—both now slashed in multiple areas with white padding pulled out. I took pictures of the devastation with my cell phone.

Waiting for the cops, it hit me: the thugs that did

this knew I'd be pulling a double today, so I wouldn't be home and they could take their time trashing the place! That meant someone at my network had tipped them off. Someone at work was helping the evil mega-corporation exposed by Emma's research, to ensure her findings stayed secret.

We had a rat in the hen house!

Emma called the next day; it was her promised weekly check-in. I had spent the morning cleaning up debris. I took her call sitting on the livingroom floor, staring glumly at my savaged couch.

When I told her what had happened, she was shocked. After first asking if I was okay, she wailed:

"They took the stick! All my research is gone! Everything I've gone through was for nothing!"

She started sobbing. So I felt I had to tell her.

"It's not all gone, Emma. I made a copy, for insurance. The assholes didn't find the copy. So your work is still safe."

The sobs subsided. There was a long silence.

"You ... you made a copy?" she finally said, snuffling.

"Yep. And it's safe."

"Oh my God! Thankyouthankyou, Bernard! Wait—did you read what was on the stick?"

"No," I lied. "Hey, I just had a thought: now that the bad guys have the stick, that should take the heat right off you. You won't have to hide anymore. You can return to Canada and get your life back."

"Y-yeah," she said slowly. "Unless they figure I made another copy, for insurance, exactly like you did, Bernard. Then they'd still want to grab me, and use coercion or torture to pry the secret out of me. Like threatening to harm—or even actually harming—my wife."

"Ah. You could be right."

"It's a horrible feeling, isn't it?" she said. "Having your home trashed like that. Now you know how we felt when it happened to our home. You feel so *violated*."

"Totally agree. The two accent pillows on my couch that they ripped open had been made by my late mother, so they're irreplaceable. You don't feel safe in your own home anymore. Last night, I jammed a chair against my door knob before I went to sleep on what was left of my mattress."

"Bernard, I'm really sorry I got you involved in this. Obviously, someone figured out that I slipped you the stick."

"This is not your fault. You needed help and I was happy to give it." Then I realized something. "Emma, if there's someone at the network who tipped off the thugs about my schedule, that means I can't give the stick to one of our news editors, if I don't hear from you each week. The story could very likely be killed."

"Good point. Well, then if it comes to that, you'll have to give it to a rival network, or maybe print media. But, as I said last time we talked, my research is incomplete. I still need hard evidence on some key areas. The powerful people involved can still wiggle out of any accusations with just the material on the stick."

"And you can't finish your research while hiding in the Outback," I said. "If you start digging again, like through a local library's computer, you'd attract the same unwanted attention."

"Yeah, I've thought of that. Honestly, I don't know what to do."

I didn't either. With shared misgivings, we hung up.

I needed to clear my head. Tomorrow was my day off. I'd go for a long ride along some of Toronto's protected bike paths.

Little did I know that it would be another life-changing ride, like the one that had prevented Dominique's initial kidnapping.

Chapter Fifteen
The Ride

The following morning, as I left my building for my usual two-hour day-off bike ride, I was stunned to see Dominique waiting. She stood next to a sweet speed machine that matched mine in performance quality.

"Wow, this is a surprise," I said, happy to see her again. "Look at you."

"Look at you too," she grinned.

We both wore skin-tight multi-colored cycling attire. She ogled my body; I did likewise with hers. Our legs were sculpted muscle. I noted her fanny pack perfectly matched the colours and design of her outfit. My fanny pack was black; it matched nothing.

"I thought it'd be fun to join you, Bernie. I wanted to do something normal with you that didn't get interrupted by an attempted abduction. You should have heard my new bodyguards! 'Oh great. Now we'll have to learn how to ride a bike!'" she laughed.

"So they're riding with us?" I asked.

"Kinda. They'll follow in a car." Dominique turned and waved to a grey SUV parked nearby.

"How'd you know about my bike ride this morning?"

"Oh, please!" she exclaimed, rolling her eyes. "Mother had you thoroughly checked out after you first rescued me. She has a file on you so detailed, it even has your elementary school report cards. We know you always take a long ride the morning of your day off."

"Hey, my shift schedule changes every week," I said.

"Yeah, but it's set for the entire month, a month in advance. You think I didn't read your file?"

I looked affronted. "A file like that is a gross violation of my privacy! That's unfair—I don't know that much about you."

She laughed again. *She had a wonderful laugh.* "I told you a bunch of stuff about me when we had dinner. So, we gonna ride, or stand here yakking all morning?"

"Okay, let's ride. Wait—aren't you supposed to be in seclusion at some cabin way up North?"

"I just got back. Bernie, I was stuck up there for three weeks. I was going stir-crazy! I spent half the day working on my MBA, and the other half learning a new skill. Now let's go!"

She took off before I could say another word. I chased her. We soon came to the entrance to one of Toronto's paved bike trails, and smoothly swerved onto it.

Side by side, we embarked on a long-distance ride. She matched me pedal for pedal. Neither of us got winded. We were both in prime shape; me from cycling daily, her from her sports, especially track and field.

Mid-way through the ride, we lunched at an outdoor roadside café near the trail. I insisted on paying this time.

"I can actually afford these prices," I said, grinning.

She laughed. "I bet the food here tastes just as good." *(She was right; it did.)*

I looked around and spotted the grey SUV.

"How'd they know where we are?" I asked. "The trail is out of sight from the road for long stretches."

Dominique patted her chest. "GPS tracker sewn into my sports bra."

"Well, at least they didn't inject you with it! I saw that in a Bond movie."

"Oh, Mother wanted one injected into me, but I put my foot down. No way."

I asked about her new bodyguards. She said they were Ilya and Anya, a man and a woman, both former Russian Special Forces who'd become disgusted by what their government was doing, and emigrated. They'd been working in Canada as bodyguards for a year. They did not come cheap.

"So I gather there's still a threat to you? The other, ah, family is still after you?"

She looked at me steadily, her blue eyes piercing. "I know about Oliver, y'know, and how Mother gifted his services to you, and how you didn't want him to do what he does best, and how you asked Mother to reassign him to terminate the bastard who ordered my abduction."

"Oh. I wondered how much you, um, knew."

"I know every detail about Mother's various enterprises."

I cleared my throat. "All her enterprises?"

Her eyes bore into me. "Yes. What, you think I'm some pampered dummy?"

"If I know anything about you, Dominique, it's that you're no dummy. Your MBA program at U of T does not accept dummies."

"Damn right."

"So, um, you're good with the nature of some of your mother's businesses?"

"I'm well aware that Mother heads a criminal empire, along with many legit businesses. How could I grow up with her and not be aware of that? But each year, for eight years now, Mother invests into more and more legit enterprises—and charities. She has been slowly divesting herself from the criminal businesses. I admire her for that. When I get my MBA, I'll help her accelerate that process until, one day, we'll be entirely legit."

I stared at her. *How do I feel about that?* "That's, um, very admirable. Thank you for being frank with me, Dominique."

"You've earned it, Bernie."

She took a long drink from her power smoothie. "In case you're wondering, Oliver hasn't fulfilled his new contract yet. In fact, he's gone dark. We haven't heard from him in a while."

"Well, I certainly haven't either. Nor will I." She looked at me quizzically, and I told her about Oliver and the garbage. She erupted into gales of laughter.

"Oh my God! Wait until I tell Mother! The King of Cool covered in garbage! Oh Bernie, you're lucky he didn't kill you!"

"Yeah." *(Damn lucky.)*

Lunch over, we remounted our carbon fibre steeds and pedalled back to where we'd started. Again, the trail had long sections out of sight of any roadway.

When two guys stood in the centre of the path, we sounded our handlebar bells. They didn't move. We braked.

"Get out of our way!" Dominique commanded. "We're riding here!"

I looked behind.

"Two more behind us!" I said.

"Shit," she said.

One guy ordered us to dismount and to not give them any trouble.

We dismounted. I laid my yellow-and-black bike down, wondering how badly I'd get pounded after I flung myself at the thugs in front of us.

Meanwhile, Dominique's hands went to the fanny pack behind her back. Then she had a gun pointed at the guy who had spoken.

"It's you and your goons who'd better not give us any trouble!" she growled. "I am fed up with being a victim. I know how to use this gun—you'll see I've flicked the safety off. So back off, or I start shooting!"

What the hell?!

Five guys all gawped at the big black gun filling Dominique's hand. It looked like it meant business. It was steady as a rock and pointed right at the gang leader's chest.

"Now take it easy, little lady," he said. He stepped back a pace. "We're not after you. Don't even know who the hell you are. We want the guy there."

"Bernie? Whaddya want with him?"

"We just wanna take him for a ride so our boss can ask him some questions. He's concerned that Bernie might still have something he shouldn't have."

Dominique glanced at me. I shrugged.

"What I said still stands," she barked. "Back off or get shot."

The gang leader snorted. "You prolly don't even know how to shoot that thing, sweetheart. That's even if it's real an' not a prop." He stepped forward.

K-CHOW! Dominique fired. The bullet plowed into the asphalt path right next to the thug's foot. He yelped and hopped back.

"That's exactly where I was aiming, you bastard. My next shot goes into you."

The leader gave some sort of signal. The four men melted into the woods beside the trail. After a long minute, Dominique replaced her gun in her fanny pack.

"Sweet Baby Jesus!" I said. "I never knew you carried a gun and knew how to use it!"

"I do now. That's the new skill I learned up North. One of my new bodyguards, Anya, is an excellent teacher. I practiced two hours every day for three weeks. She said I'm a natural. I have 95% accuracy on targets."

"Wow. You're one impressive woman."

"And don't you ever forget it," she grinned.

"Um, I haveta ask: you got a licence for that thing? I understand handgun licenses take forever to get."

"Yes, officer, I have a Possession and Acquisition

Licence, otherwise known as a PAL. It was fast-tracked. Mother has connections."

"Wait, didn't our beloved federal Liberal government make it a crime to buy or inherit handguns, as of October, 2022?"

Dominique smiled. "We knew months ahead that the new law was coming. Besides, this was a gift."

"Uh-huh."

She continued: "Hey, those assholes weren't after me this time. They were after you! What's up with that?"

I knew. It had nothing to do with her. It had everything to do with a memory stick hidden in a pound of frozen hamburger meat.

I shrugged. "Dunno."

"Well, let's get outta here before the cops show up," she said, remounting her bike. "Someone's sure to have heard that gunshot and called the police."

We rode together to her brownstone. Before saying goodbye, she said:

"I'm happy that this time I saved you, Bernie. Once more, and we'll be even!"

Then the most surprising event of the entire day occurred: she leaned over and kissed me on my cheek!

"Let Anya and Ilya report that to Mother," she giggled.

Chapter Sixteen
The Refuge

I hardly slept that night. Too many thoughts fighting amongst themselves in my tiny brain:

Whoever is after Emma is after ME now! Dominique is now armed and dangerous! Her mother is on the road to becoming completely legit—does that excuse her years as head of a criminal empire?

And the most unsettling thoughts of all: *She kissed me on the cheek! Just a friendship thing—the French do it all the time, though she's not French—or does it signify something more, that she really likes me? Do I want to get involved with a girl—woman—with mob ties?*

I finally fell asleep just sixty minutes before my alarm rang. Lucky me.

As I cycled into work along my usual route, the crisp morning air in my face keeping me awake, I wondered if that made me an easy target for whoever had tried to grab me yesterday. *Maybe I should change my route?*

I arrived without incident, though I couldn't shake the feeling I was being watched. As I was settling in at my work station, Anthony rolled in his chair over to me.

"Didja hear?" he asked.

"About what?" I answered. "They found life on Mars? We all get a four-day work week? The Avengers are moving their HQ to Toronto because of our lower dollar and some sweet tax breaks?"

"No, ya goof. The Evil Dictator will be laid up for almost a year, then he's taking early retirement. So the Suits have decided we don't need a Manager for this department after all. They'll soon advertise for a Supervisor, at a much lower salary than they paid our ED. The money they save will let you and me keep our jobs—so no layoff in this department!"

"Wow, that's wonderful news," I said. *It's exactly what I thought they should do!*

"So? You going for it?"

"For what?"

"Man, you're thick today. The new Supervisor's job! You're the most qualified one of us in the department. Nice jump in pay for ya."

"Huh. I dunno. I'll think about it." *First I have to see if I survive the next few days.*

During my break, I called Detective Kate Milllard. After some pleasantries, I asked:

"Did you get anything out of the goon from the last kidnapping attempt of Dominique in that fancy restaurant?"

"He's gone," she replied.

"Gone? You mean he also escaped your custody, like the last one?"

"No, I mean he died. He was still in a coma from that blow to the head. Yesterday, he died."

"Oh. That's too bad."

She agreed. Another lead gone. We ended the conversation.

I didn't tell her about the thugs who had tried to snatch me yesterday. It would raise awkward questions about Dominique's involvement and her having and firing a gun in a public area. I was pretty sure she had done something very illegal that exceeded the parameters of her new PAL.

I also didn't ask about police protection for myself. For that, I'd have to give details about what was on the memory stick, and Emma hadn't yet found conclusive proof that the cops could act on. So they wouldn't give me protection.

I was on my own. *Should I join Emma and her wife in the Australian Outback, cowering with the kangaroos?*

No. I had to keep working. Bills to pay. Plus there was the principle of the thing: if I ran and hid, that meant the bad guys won. *Cold comfort if you're dead, stupidhead.*

I rode home that afternoon via a different route. When I wheeled my bike into the front lobby of my apartment building, I noticed a guy across the street, watching me.

I suddenly realized the same guy had been there when I left that morning.

I decided it was perfectly okay to be paranoid.

I had been inside my apartment only five minutes when a knock came on my door. I opened it, coming face-to-face with Dominique, flanked by her two Russian bodyguards. *So much for buzzer security at our building lobby! Assassins, mobsters, and apartment destroyers, c'mon right in, no problem.*

"Hi!" I said, surprised. She was dressed in tight jeans and a plaid shirt today.

"Hi yourself," she said.

Without a word, the male bodyguard—Ilya?—pushed past me and entered my apartment. The other—Anya—stayed with Dominique, looking up and down the corridor.

"Hey, what are you doing?" I called after Ilya.

A minute later he reappeared, growling: "Clear. Is pig sty."

Dominique and Anya entered and stopped dead. "Christ, it looks like a tornado hit this place," said Dominique.

"Yeah, some bad guys tossed my place two days ago, looking for something," I said.

"Looking for what?"

"My secret Green Lantern power ring. I'm a cosmic defender, y'know."

She frowned. "I'm sure you are, Comic Book Guy. Get serious, Bernie. This have something to do with those guys on the trail yesterday?"

"Yes," I admitted. "They're after a memory stick that a work colleague gave me for safekeeping. It contains explosive info about a mega-corporation's dirty tricks and the politicians caught in its web."

"Did they find what they were after when they wrecked your place?"

"Yes."

"So that's why they want to grab you, to see if you'd made a copy?"

I nodded.

"Did you?"

I shrugged.

"Then that settles it," she said firmly. "Go pack a suitcase, Bernie. You're staying with me at my townhouse for a week, at least."

"Wha - what?"

"You heard me. You need to stay somewhere else until this is settled. So you'll stay with me. Lots of security at my place. That's if they even think to look for you there."

"But ... but..."

"No buts. I assume you have to keep working, so you can't leave town. I also assume you can't afford to stay at a downtown hotel. You have no relatives in or around Toronto to crash with. I know from our first, ah, encounter that my townhouse is on your way to work. So it'll be an ideal refuge for you."

"Thanks, and your assumptions are correct. But, um, will your mother be okay with this, um, arrangement?"

"It was her idea, after I told her what happened yesterday. I think she likes you. But don't get any funny ideas—the townhouse has a separate guest bedroom."

"*Moi?* Funny ideas? M'Lady, you wound me. I am ever a complete gentleman."

"Yeah, right. You're a male. Enough said. Now get packing."

A short time later, we were in the grey SUV, headed to her townhouse. My battered suitcase was in the trunk area; my cycle was clamped to the rear bike rack.

The watcher across the street hadn't been there as we loaded and left.

Upon arrival, we entered a private underground

garage. Stairs led to the first level. I looked at my suitcase in the trunk, then the stairs, then at Ilya.

He regarded me impassively. "Am not bellhop."

So I hauled my case up the stairs.

Reaching the foyer, I stopped and gawked. High ceilings, lots of dark carved wood, tiled floor with intricate patterns.

"Quite impressive," I said.

"Yes, isn't it?" Dominique said. "The house is over 130 years old, but has had extensive renovations since Mother bought it. We kept as much of the original decor as we could. Kitchen is state-of-the-art. Livingroom—or what used to be called the drawing room—is off the foyer here. Then the dining room, which can seat a large entourage. Kitchen is at the end of this long hall. Across the hall from the dining room is what used to be a billiards room, where gentlemen used to smoke cigars and drink port after dinner, while the ladies stayed in the drawing room and gossiped. It's now an entertainment centre, with large-screen 4D TV, video games console, and a sound system that outdoes anything you'll find in a movie theatre.

"Bedrooms are upstairs. Drag your obviously-heavy suitcase up there and I'll show you the guest room."

Up we went. I tried hiding my huffing and puffing; my case weighed a ton. The guest room was the first room at the head of the stairs. A long corridor with several closed doors led away from it.

"My room is at the end of the hall," Dominique said. "I have my own ensuite bathroom. Your room has its own bathroom too. Ilya and Anya's bedroom is mid-way down the hall, and the other doors lead to another bathroom and the linen closet."

"Wow, some place," I breathed. "Thanks again for letting me crash here."

"Happy to help, considering how you've saved me twice, Bernie. Now get yourself settled. Cook will have dinner ready in an hour."

I get home-cooked meals? Bonus!

After an excellent roast beef dinner, with wine, Dominique and I sat in the livingroom to talk. We sat on couches opposite each other.

"So tell me about the outfit trying to take over your mother's businesses," I said.

"Well," she replied, "as Mother told you, it's a foreign mob trying to muscle their way into Canada. They hail from the States, but also have ties with a big Asian outfit. Mother refuses to have anything to do with them, of course. She's defending what she and her father have built over the decades. That's why they're after me, to use me as leverage to get Mother to capitulate."

"So it's a power struggle."

"Yep. Likely will get nasty too, before too long. Trying to snatch me—twice—has made Mother furious. She retaliated by sending Oliver after the bastard responsible, but more will happen if Oliver doesn't succeed."

"So who is heading this foreign outfit?" I asked.

"The mob kingpin runs his American empire from a huge ranch in Texas. But the guy in charge of their expansion into Canada lives here in Ontario, at an estate northwest of Toronto that cost millions. He paid cash. He's already managed to establish several criminal operations here, despite Mother's best efforts. He's the one who ordered my kidnapping. He stays holed up at his estate, which he's turned into a fortress, which is why Oliver has been unsuccessful in getting to him so far."

"What's his name?"

"Javier de Sousa. A real piece of work. Cruel, sadistic, power-hungry. Misogynist bastard too. Multiple arrests in the USA, Mexico and Columbia, but nothing ever stuck. Has kept his nose clean in Canada since he arrived last year, as far as the cops are concerned."

His name sounded familiar, but I couldn't quite place it.

"Welp, I've an early class tomorrow, so I'm off to bed," Dominique announced, rising. "Tomorrow night, I expect you to return the favour and tell me why those guys are after you. Sleep well, Bernie."

I also rose. "Yeah, I'll call it a night too. Hardly slept at all last night. Thanks again for taking me in."

We both trooped upstairs, me to my room, she to hers.

What, no kiss goodnight?

There was a pair of new silk pyjamas on my bed, green, next to a luxurious white bathrobe. Of course, the PJs fit perfectly. *A not-so-subtle hint to chuck my ratty old sleepwear?*

I was just nodding off to sleep when it hit me. Where I'd seen the name Javier de Sousa before.

"Holy shit!" I exclaimed, sitting bolt upright. "Holy shit!"

I flung myself out of bed, jammed into the bathrobe, and tore open my door. I ran down the hall and pounded on Dominique's door, calling her name. After a moment, she opened the door, clad in a bathrobe with intricate gold and white designs of cranes on a pale blue background. It didn't look like she was wearing PJs underneath. She saw me staring.

"You better be staring at my robe's design, mister," she said. "It's a yukata, handmade by artisans in Kyoto, Japan."

She called past me: "It's okay, go back to bed." I turned and saw her bodyguards standing in the hall, with guns. They both glared at me, then returned to their room, Anya muttering something in Russian that did not sound friendly at all.

"What is it, Bernie?" she asked. "Why the ruckus?"

"You have to arrange a meeting for me with your mother," I blurted. "Tomorrow!"

Chapter Seventeen:
The Connection

I called in sick for work the next morning. The afternoon found me once again in Angelica's office, but with a change. This time, Dominique was with me, having finished her morning class at U of T.

En route, I had Thomas stop at my apartment so I could pick something up.

Angelica greeted her daughter warmly, with a hug and a kiss on the cheek. Me? I got a thin smile and a handshake.

She sat at her desk; Dominique and I took the chairs opposite.

"Thank you for letting me stay at your city townhouse," I said.

Angelica waved a hand. "It is nothing, Bernard. Now what is so important that you had to see me right away? I had to reschedule an afternoon commitment to see you."

Dominique added: "Yeah, what's up, Bernie? You've refused to tell me anything."

I took a deep breath. "I believe I have something that will be of great interest to you, Angelica. A colleague at work was digging into a story about corporate corruption, focusing on a well-known multi-national with offices and plants all over the world, including Canada. This corporation has powerful politicians in its pocket, has flouted tax and environmental laws with impunity, and was responsible for the Canada-wide shortage of children's over-the-counter cold and fever medicines last Winter."

"Interesting," said Angelica, "but what does this have to do with me?"

"As Emma, my work colleague, dug deeper, she uncovered hints of a major underworld connection to this mega-corporation. As she continued to dig, certain parties got wind of her research, and threatened her if she did not stop it. Ultimately, Emma had to flee Canada and go into hiding for her own safety.

"Before leaving, Emma gave me a memory stick for safekeeping with all her research. Though I wasn't supposed to, I read it. Twice. It shocked me. The levels of corruption, of secret payoffs, of illegal actions, blew my mind. The info on that stick could topple several nations' governments, including ours.

"Then, last night, Dominique told me the name of your main adversary, who's trying to muscle his way into Canada's criminal underworld and supplant your organization: Javier de Sousa.

"His name is in Emma's research!"

Angelica and Dominique both leaned forward.

"Really?" Dominique said.

"Yes. It's in the section of her research where she uncovered alleged underworld ties. She has a list of names of the key players. De Sousa's name is at the top of the key players in Canada."

"You said 'alleged'," Angelica said. "So there is no proof?"

"Not yet. Nothing the cops or government can action. Emma had to flee before finishing her digging. But there are very strong indicators—links—that tie known mob figures to this mega-corporation."

"Is my name on the list?" Angelica asked.

"No."

"This was the memory stick the culprits were looking for when they searched your apartment?"

"Yes. And they found it."

"Ah," Angelica sat back. "Well, that is it, then. Why have you bothered me with this? This has been a waste of my time."

Dominique stared at me accusingly.

"Not quite." I smiled and reached into my backpack. I brought out a plastic bag and thumped it onto Angelica's beautiful teak desk.

"What the hell?" both women blurted.

"I made a duplicate stick," I said. "I hid it in the middle

of a pound of extra lean hamburger meat that I was really looking forward to grilling. It was in my freezer and the thugs missed it."

I pointed to the frozen lump of meat. "It's in there."

Utter silence.

"Well done, Bernie!" Dominique exclaimed. Her mother nodded, eyes fixed on the meat.

"Why are you giving this to me?" Angelica said.

"It's for our mutual benefit," I said. "The cops or government authorities can't act on Emma's findings, but you can. You can start dismantling the mega-corporation, or at the very least, its mob connections in Canada. There's information there on de Sousa's Canadian operations, stuff that he very much wants to keep secret. This gives you inside intel.

"Taking him out of the picture obviously helps your organization—and keeps Dominique safe from future kidnapping attempts, or worse. For myself, with de Sousa gone, my friend Emma can come out of hiding and get her life back. His goons will stop trying to kidnap me. So it's a win-win all around."

"If the information is as you say, Bernard, then you will have again rendered me a great service," Angelica said. "Once again, you are placing me in your debt."

"Not at all. It's a service to me too, if you action the info," I said. "You're able to take action; the cops cannot since there is no hard proof. Any charges brought against de Sousa and his people will be defeated in court, if it even gets that far. But you don't need legal action to succeed."

"No, I certainly do not. Let me study this—once the meat thaws—and have some of my top people analyze it."

She rose, indicating the meeting was over. Dominique and I also rose.

"You go back alone with Thomas," Dominique said. "I have some things to do here for the next few hours."

I made my goodbyes and left.

Dominique later told me what happened after I left.

A tall shadow detached from a dark corner of Angelica's office.

"Thanks for lettin' me sit in on this meeting, Ms. Vargas," Oliver said. "I'm glad I connected with you to give a progress report. Though there weren't much progress—I haven't been able to get to de Sousa."

A humourless wolf grin split the assassin's features as he looked at the package of frozen beef.

"Good ol' Bernie. I think I can use this," he said.

Chapter Eighteen:
The Chase

"WHAT?!" she screamed. "You did what?!"

I held the phone away from my ear, wincing. Even long distance, her anger was as forceful as if she had been standing in front of me.

It was several days after my meeting with Angelica. Emma had called while I was getting ready for work; her weekly check-in with me. I had just told her what I had done with my duplicate of her stick.

"Now hear me out, Emma," I pleaded. "It's in both of our best interests."

"Don't mansplain this to me! That research was my property!" she shouted. "You had no right to give it away!"

"Emma, the bad guys after you are now after me. You know my apartment got trashed. Well, soon after that, they tried to grab me when I was out cycling. Now I'm in hiding too. You said there wasn't enough evidence for the authorities to act. But there's ample info for Angelica Vargas to act. She'll go after them—cripple them—and take the heat off us."

"I remember the news—you saved Vargas' daughter from being kidnapped. That's how you connected with her? So now you're buddies with the ruthless head of organized crime in Eastern Canada?"

"Yeah, but - "

"That's who you gave my weeks and weeks of research to?"

"Yeah, but - "

Emma screamed at me again, using profanities that would make a sailor blush. Some were so inventive, I wondered if I should write them down for my future use.

She was still venting fire when the line abruptly went dead.

I made myself a strong cup of coffee and seriously considered adding a shot of brandy to it.

I left the brownstone and took an alternate route to work. (Dominique was still in her room when I left, but I knew she'd had a late night.) Emma's reaction to what I had done with her info really rattled me. I'd been sure she would see the logic of my action, how it was our only chance of escaping de Sousa's goons.

I stopped at a traffic light. I was not one of those cyclists that barreled through red lights and stop signs as if they only applied to vehicles. *Which turned out to be unfortunate for me.*

A brown panel van pulled up beside me. Suddenly, its side sliding door snapped open and two pairs of burly arms shot out to grab me off my bike!

My peripheral vision—which was excellent—noticed them just as it happened, allowing me to crouch low over my handlebars. They grabbed at thin air. I started pedalling hard, swerving right and charging into a stream of migrating pedestrians in the crosswalk. Miraculously, I didn't hit anyone. A chorus of shouts and invectives sounded behind me.

The van had to wait until the light changed and the crosswalk was clear. Then it raced in pursuit.

I saw them coming over my shoulder. Just as they came up on me, I leaned hard over and shot down an alley. I heard a screech of brakes behind me, then the roar of an engine. The brown van was still chasing me.

But a cyclist can go where a vehicle cannot. I cut down a walkway leading away from the alley. No way a van could fit. The walkway led to an outdoor plaza bordered by streets. I tore across the plaza, upsetting office workers with steaming lattes and dog walkers with pampered "fur babies". Reaching a street, I raced away.

Safe!

The brown van shot out of an intersecting street and screeched to a stop in front of me. I braked hard to avoid face-planting into it. The side door snapped open again. This time, I saw guns pointed at me.

With a cry, I heaved the bike around so it was parallel to the van and took off. My heart sank. The street ahead was jammed with traffic. Even the bike lane was clogged—with cars.

I hopped onto the sidewalk and continued pedalling, swerving around pedestrians, who shouted the most colourful phrases. The first side street I came to, I swerved into it.

I chanced a look behind me. No van.

I turned onto a cross street, figured out where I was, and started heading for my network headquarters.

A racing engine came up fast behind me. I had seconds to react. I jammed on my brakes. The van shot past, then its brakes screeched. I pedalled down an alley, then a walkway, then across another plaza.

I was now just two blocks from my work. Its gated entrance would prevent the van from entering. Once inside its fenced parking lot, I'd be safe.

One block away, the van found me again. It came at me from a side street, aiming to hit me broadside. I swore and braked hard again. The van's front fender clipped my front wheel, and I almost tumbled off my saddle.

Recovering, I jerked my bike 180 degrees around and retreated, this time against the traffic and oncoming cyclists. Lots of swerves and near misses. Lots of swearing and uplifted middle fingers. *Sorry folks!*

My front tire was wobbly. Grimly, I kept riding. My bike was the only thing keeping me free right now. I heard sirens. *Hopefully they're after the van. Surely someone must have called this in!*

I tore down an alley, then down a cross street, heading straight for the security gates of my work. The guard in his enclosed cubicle gawped at me charging up at full speed. I skidded to a stop, slammed my employee card on the scanner, the red-and-white striped steel barrier slowly swung up, and I lurched inside.

Breathing hard from fright and exertion, I slowly rode to the bike rack at the back of the building, dismounted, and chained my bike to it.

Why is de Sousa still after me? Angelica should have started using the info on the memory stick by now, taking the heat off me.

I entered the building and was almost at Master Control when I was intercepted by Vice-President Martin Bledsoe, resplendent in another tailored suit. I was stunned. *What was a Suit doing here so early?*

"Ah, Bernard, glad I ran into you," he said. He looked like he'd just been running.

"Um, g'morning, Mr. Bledsoe," I said.

"Yes indeed. Please follow me. I want to show you something."

"Um, I have to start my shift in MC, Sir," I said. "Sarah is expecting me to relieve her after her eight-hour night shift. I know she's anxious to get home to her toddler."

"This won't take long, Bernard. Please come this way."

The Suit led me down several flights of stairs to the basement, an area I'd never been in, because I'd never had a reason to go down there. We went down a long passage. Then he opened a door and snapped on a light. I followed him into a small windowless room, piled high with boxes covered with dust.

"So what do you want to show me?" I asked.

Something stung my neck. Then everything went black.

Chapter Nineteen:
The Interrogation

I regained consciousness, feeling uncomfortable. Then I realized I was strapped to an armchair. Thick leather straps crossed my chest and stomach, pinning me to the back of the chair. My wrists and ankles were also strapped to the chair.

I then realized I was only wearing my undies. *It's like Momma always said: "always wear clean underwear when leaving home, in case you get kidnapped and stripped".*

I squirmed and fought my bonds, but they held firm.

A bright light shone on me from above. I looked around. I seemed to be in some big, empty, old warehouse. Something scuttled in the darkness. Water dripped somewhere. I certainly wasn't at my network HQ. *Though the sound of dripping water wasn't unusual.*

Martin Bledsoe sauntered into the light. He looked more like a weasel than usual.

"Ah, you're finally awake, Bernard," he said, smirking.

"Yeah. Why am I like this? Are you into some kind of kinky bondage fetish? That what you do in your fancy office all day?"

"Hah. Hah. You'd best mind your tongue. You're in no

position to be cocky."

"What the hell are you up to, Bledsoe? You drugged me, kidnapped me, stripped me almost naked—WHY?"

"There's someone who very much wants to meet you, Bernard. He requested that I bring you here. He wanted your clothes off so you would fully appreciate the damage he will do to your body if you don't cooperate. I must admit, it's too bad we couldn't get hold of Emma. I'd love to see her tied up like that in her skivvies."

Goddamn sicko!

A tall, powerfully-built man came into view. He wore the kind of rugged jacket a hunter would wear, khaki cargo pants, and heavy boots. It looked like he had come direct from a hunt camp in the bush. In perfect English, he said:

"I am Javier de Sousa, Mr. Keiler. I received your message that you had something to sell that affected my businesses, but would only sell it to me in person. If I did not meet you with the money you demanded, you would give it to the media."

I stared at him. "Wh-what?"

"Do not play dumb. What you do not know is that I react poorly to blackmail. I do the extortions, it is not done to me."

"But I never contacted you!" I bleated. "I don't even know how!"

"Yes, you did. So here I am. I understand you possess a memory stick with considerable damning information about me and my interests, that is a duplicate of a stick already in my possession, that my associates found in your apartment. You will give me that duplicate stick, Mr. Keiler, or suffer the consequences. You will also give me assurances that no other duplicates exist."

I looked past de Sousa to Bledsoe, smirking in the background.

"Bledsoe, you bastard!" I snarled. "This is how you treat your loyal employees? Emma goes into hiding and I get kidnapped?"

"So-called loyal workers should just keep their heads down and work," he sneered. "But no, you both had to cause trouble. You both refused to cooperate. Incidentally, I hope you appreciate the difficulty I went through to get you here, unnoticed by anyone, after you evaded Javier's men in the van."

"Oh yeah, I'm totally in awe," I said. "You're quite a guy."

"I'd advise you to tell him the truth, Bernard. You're a terrible liar. That's how I knew Emma had given you something when I asked you about her at work."

De Sousa smiled. "Mr. Bledsoe here is the reason I maintain a network of operatives in key Canadian businesses—to alert me if something threatens my enterprises. What is on that duplicate stick certainly qualifies."

He leaned close to me. "Surrender the stick and this unpleasantness will end."

"Look, I don't have it any more!" I shouted. "That's the truth! And I never contacted you to attempt a blackmail! I would never do that!"

De Sousa sighed. "Something else you do not know about me: I have no patience for negotiations."

From a shoulder holster under his hunting jacket, de Sousa withdrew a huge chrome gun. It made Dominique's gun look like a toy.

"This is a .357 Magnum, just like Clint Eastwood uses in *Dirty Harry*. I love that movie. This gun makes a big hole in people. I shall demonstrate."

He pressed the barrel of the Magnum to my left shoulder.

"Hey! Wait!" I shouted. "Don't!"

He pulled the trigger. *CHOOM!*

I sometimes wondered what it would be like to have skin invulnerable to bullets, like Superman or the Hulk. It sure would have come in handy today.

Pain, more intense than any I've ever experienced, tore through me. I screamed. I twisted my head to see a hole about two inches below my shoulder, leaking blood. *(My God! So much blood!)* I screamed again and seriously considered fainting.

De Sousa smiled and pressed his chrome cannon to my right kneecap. "This is where I shall fire next, Mr. Keiler. It will destroy your knee. Unless you tell me where I can get that damned memory stick, right now."

"I already told you—I don't have the stick! I never contacted you!" I yelled. "You must believe me! Please!"

He cocked the hammer of the Magnum.

"For God's sake, please don't!" I wailed.

"You know, I think I do believe you," de Sousa said. "But I will fire anyway, because you have been very troublesome. We would have had our hands on the Vargas girl weeks ago if it was not for your interference."

"NOOOO!"

A gunshot sounded. I screamed.

A small red hole appeared in the centre of de Sousa's forehead. Then the back of his head blew out, splattering Bledsoe with blood, brains, and bone.

The gangster dropped like a stone, his Magnum clattering on the cement floor.

Bledsoe stood, speechless, mouth agape. Then he fumbled in his jacket pocket and jerked out a gun half the size of Dominique's, so small it looked like a joke. He started to aim it somewhere behind me.

Another gunshot sounded. A small hole appeared on

Bledsoe's fitted blue shirt, just above his heart. (He wore no tie, per current corporate chic.) Then he too fell, joining de Sousa on the floor.

The man in black slid into view. "Thank you, Bernie boy. You were the perfect bait to flush de Sousa outta his fortress. So my contract with Ms. Vargas is satisfied. An' I'm sure you've no objection to me popping Bledsoe—I'm sure you wanted him dead, right? So Ms. Vargas' obligation to you is also satisfied."

My shoulder a white-hot pit of pain, I stared at the assassin. "You ... you used me as BAIT?"

"Yup. Figured it was the least you could do, considering that garbage incident. Didn't plan on you being shot, though. I didn't quite get set up here in time. Sorry about that."

"I've just been shot and you're sorry? That makes me feel SO much better."

"Your wound isn't fatal. The bullet went in the fleshy part of your shoulder, and came out your back. A clean through-and-through shot. You should heal up just fine, though it'll hurt like a bastard. I'll call 911 now to send an ambulance."

Oliver did so, giving the address of our location. Then he stood next to me, a wicked-looking black knife in his hand. I shrank back in my bonds.

"Don't fret, Bernie," he said. "Chill."

His knife sliced the leather straps off me, effortlessly. I hunched forward, pressing a hand to my wound, stifling a cry of pain. I felt like crying, but stubbornly refused to. *(Not in front of this killer.)*

Oliver fetched a combat first aid kit *(I see a lot of documentaries in my job)*. He pulled out two field dressings. In under a minute, he had the dressings tightly wrapped around my front and back wounds.

"That'll hold ya 'til the medics get here," he said. "No extra charge."

I glared at him and grunted thanks.

He smiled. "I've had to apply these dressings before. Sometimes to myself."

Then he injected my arm with something.

"Morphine, for the pain," he said. "Tell the medics you got a dose. But I was never here, got that? Tell the medics an' the cops that you have no idea who saved you and gave you first aid. *Capiche?*"

I nodded, then gritted through my pain: "Did Angelica and Dominique know you'd be using me as bait?"

"Ms. Vargas knew. Not her kid."

Then he melted away, leaving me with a hole in my shoulder and two bloody corpses on the floor.

Chapter Twenty:
The Dilemma

Back in the hospital again, in another private room. Another huge floral bouquet from Dominique.

Detective Kate Millard visited me on my first day. Grilled me, to be more accurate. She peppered me with questions about Bledsoe and de Sousa. Why had they kidnapped me, why did de Sousa shoot me, and who had shot them?

I told her mostly all of it, leaving out Oliver and that I had given the duplicate stick to Angelica.

"Are you sure you're telling me everything?" she asked. "It feels like you're holding something back."

"I've told you everything I can," I replied, smiling somewhat painfully.

Millard left, shaking her head, muttering that it would take some time to fit all the pieces together. She did express hope that my life would be a helluva lot calmer from now on. *No argument from me on that score!*

Dominique visited me on my second day. She seemed quite upset at my wound. As she greeted me, it looked like she was going to cry.

"Oh, Bernie," she said. "I'm SO sorry this happened to you."

"Me too," I said. "Did you know Oliver was using me as bait to flush out de Sousa?"

"No! You must believe me, Bernie. I had no idea."

"But your Mom knew."

Anger clouded her features. "Yes, she did. When I found out, after you'd been kidnapped and shot, I was FURIOUS with Mother. As the British say: 'we had quite a row'. I ... I almost hit her!"

Is she telling the truth, or is this an act?

"If you had hit her," I said, "would each of your bodyguards have felt obligated to attack each other?"

She groaned. Then she came to my bedside and grasped my right hand, the hand unconnected to the shoulder with a hole in it.

"Bernie, are you gonna be okay?"

I shrugged and immediately regretted it, wincing in pain. "The docs say I'll heal up fine, no permanent damage. But I'll have two nice scars, front and back—combat wounds, they called them."

She squeezed my hand. "I'm very, very sorry. Look, when you get discharged, you're coming back to the townhouse with me to recuperate. No arguments! Cook will make sure you eat properly as you recover."

I thanked her. I was too sore to argue and my apartment

was still a mess. Besides, I loved Cook's cooking.

Before she left, she bent and kissed me full on the lips. A long kiss. I'm sure it spiked the monitors I was hooked up to.

Two days later, I was reinstalled at Dominique's brownstone, under strict orders from the docs and her to take it easy. No strain on the shoulder. So no cycling for a while.

My first night back, we were again talking in the livingroom after dinner. Cook had surprised me with a thick gourmet hamburger made from extra lean chuck, perfectly seasoned and grilled. I laughed at her meal choice.

"So is your Mom actioning the info on that stick yet?" I asked.

"Oh yes. She's already taking steps to absorb de Sousa's operations into her own. In fact, she's doing to them what they tried to do to her."

I sat, stunned. "Hey, she was supposed to dismantle or cripple his criminal enterprises."

"She's doing just that. By absorbing them into her operations. You must remember, Mother is an astute businessperson. By giving her the stick, you gave her an incredible opportunity. She's able to take over de Sousa's interests without bloodshed or economic upheaval."

Yeah, an astute businessperson who's also a mob kingpin.

Aloud, I said:

"What about the legit businesses under the umbrella of the evil mega-corporation? The politicians and bureaucrats in their pocket?"

"Mother will slowly maneuver quiet take-overs of the Canadian businesses, adding them to her legit portfolio. The international stuff, she'll let that be, for now. Ditto the corrupt politicians and bureaucrats—except those in Canada. Those will be—ah—leveraged as and when circumstances require."

Realization hit me and I felt awful. "My God. Giving her that stick just enabled her to expand her empire, criminal and otherwise."

"Why, yes. What else did you think would happen? Mother is eternally grateful to you, Bernie."

I sat, speechless. I felt like throwing up Cook's excellent dinner.

"And on top of that," she added, "you took a bullet for our family. You could have ratted us out, but you did not. That will never be forgotten."

Dominique suddenly smiled. "And on that topic of being eternally grateful, I finally figured out how Mother could thank you. A gift I just know you'll accept."

She bounced to her feet and ran from the room. She returned minutes later.

"Here, Bernie. Please accept this from Mother as her gracious thank-you for your service—and sacrifice—to her. To both of us."

Dominique handed me a letter-sized box two inches high, made of thick cardboard. Using a penknife she handed me, I slit open the layers of tape sealing the box. I opened the box.

Inside, sealed in hard clear plastic, was a copy of the original *Amazing Fantasy # 15* comic book from 1962—the first appearance of Spider-Man. The comic had been professionally graded by the independent firm of CGC, which had then slabbed it in the hard plastic with their certification affixed. CGC had graded it a 9.0, or Very Fine/Near Mint.

I looked up, shocked. "This ... this comic in this grade, certified and slabbed, it's worth well into six figures."

She smiled. "You like?"

"Oh my God—YES! How could I even think of turning down this rare gem?"

"You'd be crazy if you did. Although Mother thinks it's crazy to spend a small fortune acquiring something that originally cost 12 cents. But I did my research, and we paid fair market value."

"I'm sure you did. I ... I don't know what to say."

"Start with 'thank you'. I'll pass it on to Mother."

"Yes, please tell her 'thank you' for me."

She crossed the room and kissed me full on the lips again.

"I told Mother you wouldn't turn this down. So, Comic Book Guy, are you wearing Spider-Man underpants?" she murmured.

"No, I am not," I said. "Don't be silly. I'm a grown man. Spider-Man undies - pfft!" *I'm wearing Iron Man underpants today.*

Later, in my room for the night with the door closed, I lay on my back in bed with my head propped up with pillows, staring at the rare vintage comic in the light from my bedside lamp. I was holding a piece of history, the comic that had launched one of the most famous heroes of the vast Marvel stable of superheroes, which today is an empire of comic books, movies, TV shows, video games, theme park rides, clothing and toys.

So am I once again a hypocrite, accepting this gift? From a mob kingpin? A notorious criminal—though nothing has ever been proved, legally.

And how do I feel about Angelica using the stick to expand her empire? She never promised she wouldn't —I just assumed she'd expose or destroy the operations. Instead, she's taking them over! In hindsight, what the hell did I think would happen? God, am I naive!

And how do I feel about Dominique? There's definitely an attraction between us. She obviously likes me. I certainly like her.

But do I want to get involved with a mobster's daughter?

There was a soft click. I looked up at the sound of my bedroom door closing; I hadn't heard it open. Dominique stood there, clad in her yukata. She smiled and padded over in bare feet to my bed.

"Put Mother's gift away, Bernie," she said quietly. "Now I have a gift for you."

She untied the matching cloth belt of her robe and shrugged out of the garment. I'd been right: she wore nothing underneath.

"Um, I'm under strict orders to take it easy," I said.

"Don't worry, my wounded warrior, I'll be gentle," she murmured, climbing onto the bed. "Just stay on your back."

The dilemma of whether I wanted to get involved with a mobster's daughter was soon resolved.

Epilogue:
Six Months Later

I stayed at Dominique's townhouse for almost a week. When I finally returned home and opened my door, I received a shock that rivaled my shock at finding my apartment trashed.

My entire condo apartment had received a make-over. Professionally painted and decorated, including carpets and drapes. All-new furniture from one of Toronto's high-end furniture stores. The latest kitchen appliances. A special tilt-up upright bike rack for *Bumblebee II* against the wall near the door. Even my late mother's two throw cushions had been expertly repaired.

On a chic hallway table by the door, was a small card. It read: "I hope you like how it turned out." It was signed with an elegant "A".

Emma and her wife did eventually return from the Australian Outback. Of course, she no longer had a job waiting for her at the network, considering how she'd abruptly left without explanation or contact with Scheduling, HR, or her boss.

She found a similar job in Research at a rival network across town, at higher pay and with better benefits.

She never spoke to me again.

For myself, I did apply for the new Supervisor position in my department—and to no one's surprise except mine, I got the job. It was a nice boost in pay, but the hours were just as long. My colleagues called me Bernard the Supervisor, or, usually, BS.

The network did not fill the Vice-President of Something position that had suddenly become vacant with Bledsoe's death. Hardly anyone attended his funeral.

Thanks to the information on the memory stick, and de Sousa's abrupt demise, Angelica was able to greatly expand her businesses, both legitimate and criminal.

To show her continuing appreciation, after five months, on my birthday, she gave me another unexpected present: another rare vintage comic book. It was the original *Fantastic Four # 1* from 1961, the comic that had started the Marvel Age of comics. Professionally evaluated and slabbed by CGC, it was graded 9.0, or Very Fine/Near Mint, and worth six figures. (Cover price: 10 cents.)

Of course, I accepted her gift. Once again, I could not resist.

Dominique and I became "friends with benefits". I kept my apartment, she continued to live in the townhouse. But we visited each other frequently. When I stayed over at her townhouse, I did not occupy the guest room.

In February, we spent a week—just the two of us (and Ilya and Anya and Cook)—at her mother's stunning beachfront villa on the idyllic island of St. Barts in the Caribbean, flying down in her private jet. I discovered

Angelica had hosted the Prime Minister of Canada and his family two weeks prior at the villa.

There, I learned to SCUBA dive. Initially, I found it terrifying, but that soon passed, becoming exhilarating.

Dominique wore a different bathing suit each day, each one skimpier than the last. I marveled at how her suits managed to stay on. Often, they did not. Mine neither.

She doesn't mind my two bullet hole scars. In fact, she says they give me a "dangerous look".

We have not had to save each other from a kidnapping in the past six months.

I have not seen or heard from Oliver, my lethal shadow, in the past six months. But that doesn't mean he's not still out there ...

The End

About The Author

Since 2003, **BRUCE GRAVEL**'s light-hearted stories have delighted readers of newspapers like the *Peterborough Examiner*, *Peterborough This Week*, and the *Globe & Mail*, and magazines like *Maclean's* and *Association*, among others.

His first book, **Humour on Wry, with Mustard**, a collection of 88 whimsical tales, was published in 2008.

His second book and first novel, **Inn-Sanity: Diary of an Innkeeper Virgin**, was published in 2009.

His third book, **Humour on Wry, with Mayo featuring Travels with Fred, the World's Worst Tourist**, collecting 51 witty yarns appeared in 2010.

In 2012, **Humour on Wry with Ketchup** was published,

featuring 32 amusing stories.

In 2015, Bruce shifted gears, releasing **The Hero Stone**, a fantasy adventure novel for readers aged 13 and up, starring three teenagers, including one living with an intellectual disability.

In 2019, **Humour on Wry, with Salsa** was published, a collection of 69 funny short stories (and a recipe for rhubarb salsa!).

Humour on Wry, with Relish appeared in 2021, featuring 84 quirky short stories (and a 100-year-old recipe for green relish!).

He currently writes a weekly humour column for the *Peterborough This Week* newspaper and online at *MyKawartha.com*.

Email him at: bruce@brucegravel.ca
Web site: brucegravel.ca

Also available:

HUMOUR ON WRY, WITH MUSTARD
88 Tasty Treats to Feed Your Funny-bone
The first book in the "Condiment Series"

Bruce Gravel's wonderful debut book of 88 short stories, that is guaranteed to cause smiles, chuckles, snorts, guffaws, and even some belly-laughs, with funny tales of everyday life. {There are cartoons too!}

To order, visit **www.brucegravel.ca**. Also available at **www.amazon.com**, including as e-book on Kindle.

"The story about eating dessert first cracked me right up!"
— Colleen Isherwood, Editor, ***Canadian Lodging News***

"I would like to complain about that 'I, Robot' story. It caused me to pull a muscle in my cheek from laughing so hard."
— Letter to the Editor of the ***Globe & Mail***

Also available:

HUMOUR ON WRY, WITH MAYO
featuring Travels with Fred, the World's Worst Tourist
The second book in the "Condiment Series"

Bruce Gravel's collection is two books in one. Book One is Travels with Fred, the World's Worst Tourist, in 21 hilarious tales of the traveller from hell, most based on true events. Book Two is 30 other funny short stories that will chase your blues away. {There are cartoons too!}

To order, visit **www.brucegravel.ca**. Also available at **www. amazon.com**, including as e-book on Kindle.

"Your Fred stories are absolutely outrageous! To a frequent traveller, there are lots of 'Freds' out there, but they are not half as entertaining as this curmudgeon."
> — Dr. Marion Joppe, Professor, School of Hospitality
> & Tourism Management, University of Guelph

Also available:

HUMOUR ON WRY, WITH KETCHUP
32 short stories guaranteed to give you giggles

The third book in the "Condiment Series"

Bruce Gravel's collection of funny stories, which will lighten your life, includes another section featuring Fred, The World's Worst Tourist. There is also a bonus section: "Humour on Wry, with Wasabi", containing two "spicy" tales. {There are cartoons too!}

To order, visit **www.brucegravel.ca**. Also available at **www. amazon.com**, including as e-book on Kindle.

"Most entertaining and well written! When I want a chuckle, I will reach for your book."

— Vena Johnstone, retired innkeeper

Also available:

HUMOUR ON WRY, WITH SALSA
69 short stories to bring you smiles & chuckles
The fourth book in the "Condiment Series"

Fun stories of misadventures and silly moments, such as: Honeymooning in the sewers of Paris ▪ How not to terminate an employee ▪ The perils of fishing naked ▪ What happens if hell is cancelled ▪ Looking for a Galway hooker ▪ Ghostly matrimony. Plus more tales of Fred, the World's Worst Tourist! (And a yummy recipe for rhubarb salsa!)

To order, visit **www.brucegravel.ca**. Also available at **www.amazon.com**, including as e-book on Kindle.

"Your 'Ginger Gang' *story is* ABSOLUTELY DELIGHTFUL!"

— Dwayne James, Artist

"Your 'Terminated at Timmy's' *story had me LAUGHING FOR 10 MINUTES!"*

— A Human Resources Manager

Also available:

HUMOUR ON WRY, WITH RELISH
84 whimsical & quirky short stories
The fifth book in the "Condiment Series"

A tongue-in-cheek look at things in life we can all relate to, such as: Bambi's revenge ▪ A murder of crows ▪ An elephantine tushy-burp ▪ The best-dressed kangaroo in Australia ▪ How to write your own tombstone ▪ The Double-0 support group ▪ True ghost stories.

20 questions for: God, the Devil, Cupid, Medusa, Death, and others!

Plus a special section: Humour in a time of virus. Craziness during the COVID-19 pandemic!

Also: More tales of Fred, the World's Worst Tourist!

Bonus: A grandmother's 100-year-old recipe for green relish!

"Bruce has mastered the twist of a phrase, the tease of suspense, and the desire to open the reader to his imaginary world of MISADVENTURES AND SILLY MOMENTS."
—Lois Tuffin, Former editor-in-chief, Peterborough This Week

"Your 'Bambi's Revenge' story is identical to an occurrence at our hunt camp! I was the doctor involved. VERY FUNNY READ."
—Dr. Paul A., who got speared

Also available:

HUMOUR ON WRY, WITH HONEY
80 delightfully funny short stories
The sixth book in the "Condiment Series"

To order, visit
www.brucegravel.ca.
Also available at
www.amazon.com,
including as e-book on Kindle.

Also available:

INN-SANITY:
DIARY OF AN INNKEEPER VIRGIN
A novel of sex and silliness, tragedy and triumph,
and exploding concrete

Bruce Gravel's debut novel incorporates hundreds of true-life incidents from actual innkeepers to hilariously, and sometimes poignantly, chronicle the crazy first year of two middle-aged novice innkeepers. Such as: A horse in a motel room! An exploding swimming pool! Giant mutant animals! A Hollywood movie shoot from hell! Saucy walls! A ghost!

To order, visit **www.brucegravel.ca**. Also available at **www.amazon.com** including as e-book on Kindle.

"The book is super! I was thoroughly engaged and had lots of laughs too."

— Colleen Isherwood,
Editor, *Canadian Lodging News*

"A great read and very interesting. Wow, hard to believe the stories are based on real events!"
— Kim Litchfield, Corporate Account Manager, WSPS

Also available:

THE HERO STONE
What if you could become your favourite superhero?

Bruce Gravel's second novel is a modern fantasy adventure of superpowers and terror, starring three brave teens, one of whom lives with an intellectual disability, confronting one depraved villain.

Does good always prevail over evil?

Meet Michael Johnson, a seventeen-year-old with the mind of an eight-year-old. An avid comic book reader, Michael finds an uncanny stone that lets his superhero fantasies become real. It also makes him a target, sending him on a cross-Canada trek, just one step ahead of a twisted, merciless predator. Michael's two teenage friends, Billy and Melanie, get swept up in his grim adventure, at great personal cost. Melanie, a strong self-reliant girl, must cope with a devastating loss.

To order, visit **www.brucegravel.ca**. Also available at **www.amazon.com** including as e-book on Kindle.

"I stayed up late into the night reading 'The Hero Stone' on my vacation. I was riveted. You got right inside the heads of the three protagonists, including Melanie. The insects and snakes scene was quite compelling!"

— Colleen Isherwood, Editor, ***Canadian Lodging News***